NIGHT IN DELHI

Praise for Previous Books

'*Dark Star* is a profound, lyrical novel about displacement and homecoming, from a writer always reinventing the possibilities of fictional form.'

—Siddhartha Deb, author of *The Light at the End of the World*

'*Dark Star* is a remarkable book. It is among the best I have read for a long time.'

—Ranjana Sengupta, *The Hindu*

'Sidhu's short and profound book shows how far English can be taken. *Dark Star* is a woman's book written by a man, a mother's by a son. For Indian writing in English, it is a huge leap.'

—Rajesh Sharma, *The Tribune*

'*Dark Star* is an important intervention that opens up new terrains for understanding the nature of intergenerational memory, mourning, and transformation in the wake of historical trauma.'

—Amandeep Caur, *The Book Review*

'Sidhu writes with keen wit and crafts every character with psychological texture, exploring the effects of racism as well as the desire to control a world spinning off its axis. *Deep Singh Blue* is a heart-wrenching coming-of-age tale in which survival depends more on compassion than rebellion.'

—*Kirkus Reviews*

'Ranbir Sidhu's debut novel *Deep Singh Blue* is an ambitious stab at a truly challenging art form. No shortcuts here, just good solid writing about flawed humans and the messes they get into.'

—KQED

'*Deep Singh Blue* is no picturesque coming of age. In an immigrant family and an adopted land both straitjacketed by denial and rage, it's an open question—and a propulsive one—whether Deep Singh's lashings out to save himself will lead to salvation or destruction. A work of ferocious bravery, intelligence, and art.'

—Alex Shakar, author of *Luminarium*

'Achingly merciless, London-born author Sidhu's 12 short stories in *Good Indian Girls* sharply delineate the edges of identity and sanity. These haunting tales simultaneously attract and repel, enchant and shatter, evoking the ambiguous relationships between past and present, others and self. Deftly sifting through a range of less-often-visited emotions, Sidhu creates inscrutable characters inhabiting bewildering circumstances. Smart, provocative and poignantly disturbing, this collection, the author's U.S. debut, signals a writer to watch.'

—*Kirkus Reviews* (Starred Review)

'Though weird and eccentric, Sidhu's stories in *Good Indian Girls* are also empathetic and refreshingly free of the clichés of immigrant narratives. He manages to portray his characters as uniquely Indian without losing sight of their individuality, offering small, piercing looks into the humanity that resides in every situation and person, no matter how strange.'

—*Publishers Weekly*

'"Border Song"—among the lightest pieces in *Good Indian Girls*—finds transformative grace in grief and a closure of sorts that eludes characters in "The Order of Things", a masterpiece of a story that could have you marvelling at Sidhu's incisive and distinctive perspective for the Punjab experience of violence, exile and estrangement—both within India and abroad.'

—Shalini Mukerjee, *Outlook*

'With adeptly drawn characters, Sidhu demonstrates a dexterous grasp of the human psyche, while the prevalence of dark twists displays his love of the fatalistic. This propensity for the morose will be off-putting for some but is sure to please those with a taste for black humor and shades of the diabolical.'

—*Booklist*

'Whenever I pick up a story by Ranbir Sidhu, I feel as though I've been released from the cedarwood closet of literature into the fresh air of active creation; as though I'd been fitted with brand-new high-tech earphones picking up an infinity of eloquent microphones cleverly scattered around the world. The pops and squeaks of new life crackle in my ears, and even when they're threatening or saddening, I'm inevitably overcome by the hope that they'll never stop.'

—Harry Mathews, author of *My Life in CIA* and *The Journalist*

NIGHT IN DELHI

antxi

RANBIR SIDHU

cntxt

Published by Context, an imprint of Westland Books, a division of Nasadiya Technologies Private Limited, in 2024

No. 269/2B, First Floor, 'Irai Arul', Vimalraj Street, Nethaji Nagar, Alapakkam Main Road, Maduravoyal, Chennai 600095

Westland, the Westland logo, Context and the Context logo are the trademarks of Nasadiya Technologies Private Limited, or its affiliates.

Copyright © Ranbir Sidhu, 2024

Ranbir Sidhu asserts the moral right to be identified as the author of this work.

ISBN: 9789360451370

10 9 8 7 6 5 4 3 2 1

Typeset by Mukul

Printed at Parksons Graphics Pvt. Ltd

For Lynne Tillman

I call you Orphan, orphan.
                    —Sylvia Plath

Look well at me. I am your Beatrice.
How dare you weep up here? Did you not know
this Paradise is made for happiness?
                    —Dante's *Purgatory*,
                    translated by Alasdair Gray

1

When Jaggi walks in he unzips his fly and produces his penis. He flashes it at me with that grin of his. I know what he's going to do and I know there's nothing that will stop him. I still call out, Don't! He turns his back on me and pisses onto the battered stone floor. A yellow pool spreads out from his feet. Instantly, the smell touches everything, and I ask him, Why do you do this, why do you make where we live a toilet, worse than a toilet? I know why but it doesn't help. The washroom is only feet away. Three steps and he'd be there. It's not exactly a large room. The grin broadens across his face and he lets out a sigh. Along with the urine, I smell the alcohol belching deep from inside him. I haven't seen him for two days. I usually wait three before I start to worry. When he was gone a week I lost my mind. No calls, no replies to messages. Then he appeared, dressed in a full-length pink overcoat, obviously brand new, with a fake fur collar, also pink, looking every inch like some oversized confection. He strutted up and down the Main Bazaar for a few days dressed like this, in the middle of May, when the city was scorching hot, walking like the very raja of Paharganj. Or some pimp out of one of those 1970s New York movies. Another week passed and the coat vanished. He never said where he'd got it from or where it went. Jaggi's silences are always larger than his words. I can spend days puzzling over them, like a monk trying to decipher a lost language. I saw the tatters of that coat months later. It was wrapping a couple and their infant child as they slept on a highway median, heads and feet sticking out into speeding traffic.

He shakes his penis, letting the final drops drip from the head, zips his pants, and walks across to the taped up photograph of Shah Rukh Khan. Shah Rukh is wearing a fedora and smoking a cigar. Jaggi treats it like a mirror, adjusting his invisible fedora and taking a few puffs from his invisible cigar. He seems satisfied, nods at himself, and turns and tilts his head back and begins to hum, an old song, from one of those old films that no one watches anymore. My anger finally ebbs, because his voice is beautiful, it carries me away, it always does, and I think how can I be angry at this man. I watch as he moves his body, dancing with himself, ignoring me completely. His head twists, eyes closed, his arms like soft currents of air, and I sit mesmerised. The stink disappears, so does the room, the city along with it and all its people with their noise and rage. What's left is Jaggi, dancing before me, a vision piercing through from a different world.

The door opens and Basam walks in and smells the air and sees the pool of urine on the floor. He doesn't hesitate. He charges straight for Jaggi and throws him to the ground, punching him hard in the face. I watch from my bunk, irritated the spell is broken and knowing how it will end. Jaggi throws Basam off, stands, and brings his great foot through the air and down onto Basam's head. I know Jaggi's kick well. He pulls himself up short right at the last second, to stop himself from crushing Basam's skull. He holds his foot in mid-air before almost playfully punching Basam's nose with it. Still, there is blood everywhere, and Basam yells and drags himself away, his hands cradling his bleeding nose. He sits in a corner, hunched and furious, blood covering his shirt. Jaggi turns away and glances towards me, a look of triumph in his eyes, and returns to his dance, humming that old tune once again. But this is Delhi now, Delhi now and always. All other worlds are gone. I throw Basam a rag and he presses it to his face, and I think, one day, one night, someone will kill Jaggi in his sleep, and maybe I am the only man who will mourn his loss. Sometimes I'm not even sure if I will.

Basam says the same thing to me, One night someone's gonna kill the bastard motherfucker. I've filled a bucket with water and am mopping the floor while Jaggi snores above us from his bunk. It will take five men, Basam says, four to hold him down and one to stab him in the heart or slit his throat or both. The blood has dried on Basam's upper lip and his nose looks twisted, more twisted than it did before. Basam says it won't be him, he's leaving, he's found a job in Gurgaon, night guard at one of those shitty rich people buildings, those crap new ones everyone knows are gonna fall down in ten years because they cheaped out on sand for the concrete. Those rich bitches are creaming for real dick, he says, not fucking middle-class-doctor-lawyer-who-gives-a-fuck dick who sits there all night watching fucking Porntube 'til his pathetic pencil for a dick's bleeding. He's gonna be pounding deep into those rich bitches, every night, he says, front behind down their throats all the way out the other end. He keeps talking, mostly about how all of Gurgaon's gonna taste his cum. I drop the mop, sit on my bunk and light a cigarette and tune him out until he gets to his point, which I've been waiting for.

He needs a shawl, he says, and shirts. Not a shit shawl, he needs something special, and real shirts, Brooks Brothers, that shit, something that'll make him stand out to the bitches, put them on notice, a serious piece of dick has entered the picture, make their holes weep just thinking about him. He keeps talking, like he often does, and I'm thinking stealing a shawl is not like picking a pocket. When you steal a shawl off someone's back, that someone notices. You have to find a shawl that no one is wearing, and as importantly, no one is watching. I say this and Basam encourages me, I can do it, he knows I can, I'm the best, that's why he lets me stay, why he tolerates Jaggi, even after shit like this. He points to his nose. He keeps talking about how good a thief I am, and I shrug, I don't know, I'm okay. Maybe a foreigner, I say, who's bought one as a souvenir, they often put the bag down when they're drinking tea, I might steal it then. Basam nods, that's the time, the perfect time, when they're downing their shitty chai lattes. We don't talk about the shirts, that's harder, but I let it pass and hope Basam will forget.

Jaggi wakes, stretches. He makes a lot of noise when he wakes, a true symphony of bodily sounds. He climbs down from the bunk and takes my water bottle and throws water onto his face and drinks some, letting the water spill across his lips and neck. He screws the top back on the bottle and throws it onto my bunk and looks at the blood on Basam's face and smiles, then looks at me and nods. Okay, he says, I'll piss outside, and he walks outside and we can hear him on the terrace as he lets out a long stream. I shout after him, There's a toilet in here, but he ignores me. After a minute, he walks back inside, still holding his penis, and points it at Basam. It will take more than five, he says. He zips up and walks out and we hear the flimsy terrace door open and close and then silence, or not silence, the noise of the city, and the smell, and Jaggi's muffled footsteps as he disappears down the stairs. After

5

he's gone, something of him lingers in the air, an aroma, a bruise, a sense of dislocation.

2

It's Jaggi's idea, he was here last week, a young woman, a suicide. The food is better when it's a suicide, he says. The mother was crying all over the place but each time she came by the kitchen she'd start abusing the cooks, cooks she'd hired specially. It has to be the best you've ever cooked, she said, the best for my daughter, my dead daughter in heaven, on and on she went about her dead daughter, Jaggi said, and the whole time whacking the cooks on the back, on their heads, he had to stop himself from laughing it was so funny. Everyone was saying it was the dead girl's time, Jaggi spits, then laughs, her time, when is it ever time for a teenage girl to die, he says. These people, he says, with their money and their houses. He got a watch, a Rolex, a real one, he promised, but that was all he could get. When I looked at it I showed him it was fake, pure Chinese crap. Maybe he could sell it to a tourist. I should've known, cheap bastards all the way, he said, and threw it on the floor and brought his bare foot down, smashing the glass and cutting his skin. I hate fake shit, he said. That was why he wanted me to come along, together the two of us could really score.

We climb white marble steps and throw our chappals into the pile with the others and tie handkerchiefs around our heads to cover them. Before walking inside, we wash our feet in a shallow pool. I like the sensation of water on my toes, but Jaggi splashes through, walking confidently into the white marble edifice. The sun shimmers against the stone and I look up to admire the gurdwara's elegance. In the cool fall light I can almost see right through the stone to the grey sky beyond. Inside, the granthi sits cross-legged under a bright pink and yellow phulkari and waves a chaur over the holy book as he recites. I pull a battered ten-rupee note out of my pocket and when I matha tek I drop it into the collection box. Jaggi does the same, except instead of falling onto all fours and quickly bowing, like me, he stretches out on the floor, his head pressed into the carpet and his arms reaching forward, towards the granthi. He lies like this for half a minute and a queue forms behind him. Then he stands, deposits not ten rupees but a hundred-rupee note, and brings his hands together in a bow. When he joins me on the carpet he winks as if to deliberately break the spell of his religious piety.

A framed photograph of the dead man is suspended on an easel at the front, still wrapped in the plastic the printers delivered the frame in, along with the protective cardboard corners. He's a good-looking sardar, in his turban and neat beard. Under the photo it shows the years he lived. He was in his eighties when he died. When I think of people that old I think of the world they were born into, another India, not mine, and think some people have luck and others don't. That photograph will hang like that for years, perhaps still in its plastic with the protective corners, in a room high on a wall, where no one can reach it. A dead man watching over his family, if that's what dead men do. The gurdwara is half full, more men than women, and most people are talking quietly. A few of the men sit reverently. The granthi stops and lays the whisk down and covers the book with another phulkari and the musicians tune up and start. I like the music, I always have, these sardars know their tunes, and soon I am drifting, letting it lull me. For a moment I am drugged, giddy, lost, floating close to the ceiling, watching the congregation below. Men, women, children, lives twisted around each other as they watch and fidget and whisper and gossip. I can almost tell myself I'm one of them. With a home, a family. In another life maybe. I rest a hand on Jaggi's lap and am briefly happy, if happiness is a thing I have ever known.

3

A turbaned figure moves through the hall, a kirpan hanging from an age-battered belt, and distributes prasad from a metal bowl. I accept it, taking the warm, sticky sweet in my fingers, and bring my hands together in thanks and eat it quickly. Jaggi shakes my shoulder. It's time to go to work, he whispers, but just then one of the old men, who is sitting near us, stands and walks stiffly over. A thin, straggly beard reaches down to the middle of his belly. He leans forward, holding himself upright with a cane, and tells us boys, as he calls us, that the langar has started, we should get something to eat. You didn't know the dead man, he adds, I can tell, so what are you doing here? He means in the hall, there was no reason for us to show respect, they'd be happy to feed us either way. He doesn't hide his irritation, scolding us for wasting our time on empty gestures when we should be filling our bellies. Come come, he demands. We rise and follow him. The musicians play. The old men are on their feet and children run in and out squealing.

The old man settles us down on a length of weathered carpet in the centre of the courtyard, a prime spot. Some women sitting opposite smile and nod in approval. A boy, maybe ten, appears with water, and is quickly followed by others, each bearing something different, dal, chole, sabzi, roti, dahi. The man distributing the roti is well-dressed, in his fifties, one of the sons of the dead man, performing seva for his father. After he drops a fresh roti onto my plate he pauses and stands there. You've read that? he says. He gestures to the book poking out of my trouser pocket with a nod of his head. I say yes and shrug my shoulders, as if to say sure but who cares. Find me later, he says, and moves on. The food was better last week, Jaggi whispers, this one just died of old age, there's no shame in that. He calls over one of the boys for more sabzi and eats hungrily, while I haunt the crowd with my eyes, searching for bulging pockets, watches loose on wrists, phones or purses left unattended.

I finish eating and find the son of the dead man. He looks at me coldly. His shirt collar is frayed and flecks of roti cling to his jacket. The jacket looks off the rack and cheap, and he looks like he can afford much better. Prove it, he says without explanation. I ask him what he means and he says that I know what he means, and I do know, so I say, almost barking the words back at him, in English, You taught me language and my profit on it is that I know how to curse! He laughs and claps me on the back. So you didn't just steal the Shakespeare, he says, and I say, Does it matter? He produces his wallet, a thick one, black and shiny, the leather frayed from age, like his collar, and pushes his card into my hand. Mr Harbans Singh Ahluwalia, Esq., embossed in gold. It shows an address in Karol Bagh. I'll call you Caliban, he says, or is that your friend, and you're Ariel. He nods across to Jaggi. He adds, It doesn't matter, they were both just slaves.

His gaze rests on me for a second too long, evaluating me too obviously. His upper lip twitches. I know what he's thinking. He points to the card and says, Meet me there tomorrow, whatever time suits you, I don't know what time you types get up. His lip curls in disgust. I know that curl. He will fuck me from behind, and when he comes he will burst into tears of self-loathing and self-pity. He adds, It's not my home, so dress how you like.

When I turn to leave, he takes hold of my shoulder. His grip is powerful, his fingers dig painfully into my flesh. He pulls me towards him and whispers, Don't steal too much, and nothing from my family, except my sister. He signals who she is with his eyes. She is sitting, surrounded, huge, dressed in a bright pink sari, talking loudly with a teary-eyed expression while devouring a piled high plate of jelabis and other sweets. Fuck her, he says, and claps me again jovially on the back and sends me on my way. I spot Jaggi from where I am. As I approach, I see his pockets. One is already full.

4

The sister is easy. People like her never see people like me. It's so simple: become invisible. An invisible man can steal anything. It's one of the tricks I had to learn, tell myself I was always poor, lose myself to other people's ideas of caste and their blindness to anyone who isn't one of them. To vanish in front of women like this. She holds court, chattering away, what a great man her father was, how saintly, how honest, how generous, on and on she goes, a man who never had a bad thought in his head, not even as a child, not even as a baby, taken away in his prime, at eighty-seven, she lets out a shriek and throws her hands into the air when she says his age, so young, so youthful! What cruel God, etc, she cries, and I pretend not to watch, not to hear, instead my attention lingers on the cooks dropping chapatis onto tavas and puffing them over the flames. Smoke rises and engulfs their faces while in the dark, under the tent set up for the cooks, a row of middle-aged women roll out the flatbreads and pat them between their hands.

The sister is still talking and no one interrupts. Her flesh heaves under her sari with each tortured breath as she damns a worthless God for letting her saint of a father die. It's too easy. Her eyes pass through me as I approach. Not only am I invisible, I don't exist, I might as well be dead, a ghost, a spirit in the air, the way her brother called me Ariel from the play. I'm heading back into the gurdwara and just as I pass I slightly trip and snatch the purse from her bag. Her eyes flash in my direction, but I can see even then that I'm not there, that she registers me as a non-entity, if she registers me at all. Not one of her sycophants dares look in my direction, no doubt out of fear of the shame a single, accidentally returned glance in my direction might bring. In such situations, shame is always my ally. I walk inside, the purse under my shirt pressed against my belly, and listen for a minute as the music unspools, then outside again and catch Jaggi's eye. I signal it's time to leave, best not test our luck. Out of the corner of an eye, I watch the brother watching me. Even from that angle I can see he's not interested in what I stole, it's me that interests him, or my body.

We buy ice creams near India Gate and eat them lying on the blasted grass, more brown than green, or grey like everything else. The sky is grey, so is the air, while the sound of construction rumbles from all sides. Everywhere they are building something, another India rises out of the earth around us. A new Parliament, for a newly born grey India, where the air is thicker than fog. I lay my head on Jaggi's lap and light a cigarette and blow smoke up and he says one day we'll go south, to Goa or Kerala, to the beaches and the easy life. A little more money, a few more purses. He takes the cigarette from my lips and blows smoke down into my face. I wonder what it would be like to kiss him here, in the open, in the crowd, with everyone watching, the new Parliament, the grey sky, all of it acknowledging such a simple thing as a kiss. He plays with my hair and a businessman hurries past and shoots us a look of hatred.

My phone beeps and I get a text. r u free. I send back a thumbs up and tell Jaggi I have to go. Which one? he says matter-of-factly. The European, I tell him. He says I never charge enough and I take the cigarette back. Smoking it is like a kiss. I stub it out and walk away and look back from the auto-rickshaw stand to see Jaggi lying on his back, hands clasped behind his head, staring up into the oblivion that is a Delhi sky. I tell the driver Jangpura and soon we are booming along the boulevards. The vehicle has a new engine and it feels like we're punching through the traffic. The horn blasts continually, as if it's set to never stop, while warm, afternoon air slaps in from all sides. He drops me at the colony gates. The guard eyes me with suspicion while his hand tightens around his lathi stick. I walk over and ask where so and so address is, though I know exactly where it is. The European professor's house, I say helpfully, and he relaxes ever so slightly. This way then that way, he says, pointing me in a totally wrong direction. I thank him and walk on, precisely following his directions which lead me around a fenced-in park. A group of maids, dressed in cheap saris, exercise on communal equipment. I circle back when the guard can no longer see me. The leaves of trees are covered in thin layers of dust, so they appear speckled, as if diseased. A yellow dog follows me, snarling, its nose at times edging against my calf, until it grows bored and disappears under the shade of a car.

5

I tell Anders I need a shower and he says no, he likes the tang of my sweat. He uses that word tang, not taste. Take it after, he says, and I lie back on the couch and accept a joint. Anders is drinking vodka, which he offers me but I refuse. I want to be clear-headed, at least a little. The apartment is sparsely furnished, the heavy curtains drawn so you can't tell if it's night or day. It's always like this, sunk in a perpetual dusk. A coffee table is piled with books. Computer science, robotics, advanced mathematics, artificial intelligence. There are books everywhere, on shelves, in piles, even in the bathroom there are books on surprising subjects, like dreams and fairy tales. He's not a professor, but anyone with so many books is always a professor. I don't even know if he's European, I just call him that. He says he can't say what he does, it's secret. I like the mystery it gives him, and because of that a sense of danger surrounds our meetings.

I take a few drags on the joint and Anders finishes his drink and unzips my pants and takes my penis into his mouth. I light a cigarette and smoke as he sucks me off and slowly I begin to melt. My body sinks into the couch and I become water, or air, I don't know what. Anders works my cock and I stub out the cigarette and close my eyes. Then I open them and lean forward and watch his head moving methodically up and down. I wait for my moment, when he's totally lost in the task, and knee him hard in the belly. He flies back and I kick his chest and throw him to the floor. I'm on him in a flash, my arm wrapping his neck and squeezing with all my strength. He kicks at me uselessly and I hear him gagging, struggling to breathe. Suddenly, he lands an elbow hard in my ribs and I double over in pain, releasing him. He jumps on top, and starts punching me, first in the chest then the belly. I kick back, slapping the soles of my feet against him. The coffee table overturns and books go thundering across the marble. He is bigger than me, and stronger, but increasingly he pulls his punches when he strikes back. I don't pull mine. I'm paid not to. This is the reason Jaggi says I don't charge enough. There should be a rough sex surcharge, Jaggi says. It's all sex to me, rough or not, and soon we are struggling across the floor, me pulling Anders' pants down as he attempts in a sort of ham-fisted way to throw me off, both of us knowing he'll fail, that eventually he'll do what he desperately wants, which is succumb to my violence.

I throw him onto his face and push his nose into the marble and enter him from behind. His body jerks violently then relaxes and I take his dick in my hand and work it hard while I bite the back of his neck. I lift my elbow and use it to press his neck painfully into the marble as I push inside. He gathers his strength and throws me off and we are struggling again, wrestling on the cool floor. This goes on for some time and we work through all sorts of bodily permutations. At the end, he fucks my face and comes in my mouth, then lets his body collapse onto me. His hips crush my head while his dick is pushed deep into my throat. I can't breathe and gag and try to push him off but he doesn't move. Only when he hears

16

me choking does he relax his weight. He grunts, smiles, and turns his attention to my dick, and finishes me off with his mouth. I tell him it's not necessary but he always does this, some point of pride, that somehow it makes us equal or who knows what. I think it's about power. The one who doesn't come has all the power. He would never give me that.

When we're finished, I take my shower and walk back in with a towel wrapped around my waist. He's still naked, with a fresh vodka in his hand. This time I accept the drink and drop the towel and collapse beside him on the couch.

6

He saw me last night, he says, on the street not far from Lodhi Gardens, and wondered what I was doing, was going to say hello but stopped himself. I was walking, I tell him, and leave it at that, and he lights another joint and passes it across. I take a long drag and pour myself another vodka. He is not handsome and it is impossible to say how old he is, maybe thirty, maybe fifty. He has the kind of face that vanishes in a crowd. I like that about him, that even as a gora he can disappear. He switches the television on and flips through channels until he finds cartoons, Looney Tunes from the fifties or sixties. After sex he always watches cartoons, sometimes modern ones, sometimes old ones. If he can't find anything on cable he pulls out a box of old DVDs and plays one at random. He leaves the sound down, he always leaves the sound down when watching cartoons, he says he sees more that way, gets deeper into the action.

I lie back, stoned, and fall against him. He hasn't showered and I smell both of us on him, our sex thinned to the glisten of his skin. The edges of the world soften, and he talks, as he sometimes does, about subjects that make little sense to me. Sometimes I think this is the reason he wants me here, so he can talk after sex about things that matter as we watch soundless cartoons. He asks what I know about myth and I say I know nothing about myth though I don't know if that's true. Myths tell you all you need to know about a people, he says, look at the Irish myths, they go deep in time, how in all those myths a hero travels from island to island, from land to land, ever restless. And who are the Irish if they're not ever restless? And the English, he says, and says there are no English myths, they were all destroyed when the English were conquered a thousand years ago, the storytellers killed, the scrolls burnt, the myths lost, and that says more than anything. Why, I say, and he says look at the English today, the most hungry people on the planet, searching for a land to conquer to fill the emptiness inside because their myths were lost long ago.

And India, I say, and he says it's a land with more myths than any other, more even than China, that maybe that's what brought him here, all the competing stories, every myth cancelling another myth, each story tying itself up in knots as it tries to outdo another, and on and on. He must know what he's talking about because I've seen his bookcases, filled and overflowing with books on mythology and religion. He talks like this for some time, as one after another cartoons play on the television. Later, as we always do, we have sex again, but not like before, it's gentler the second time, softer, more nuanced. It's almost like actual lovemaking. When I come, I come inside him. He never allows me to use a condom and I don't question him. I never ask questions like that, but wonder to myself why he has a death wish, a rich man like him, intelligent, educated.

I don't tell Jaggi about the second time, only the first. It seems wrong to make some version of real love to a man when you're in love with another. I know Jaggi doesn't care, he'd laugh at me, but I care. This is what I should be charging more for, not the rough sex, but the intimacy. The tips Anders gives more than make up for what I don't charge. This time he says the tip will be more generous. He wants me to do something for him. He disappears and reappears rolling before him what looks like a drinks cart, but instead of bottles it holds a machine with a screen and different coloured buttons and knobs. What is it? I say and he says it's for his work, it'll record my neural patterns, if I agree. Sure, I tell him, and lie back into the couch cushions while he attaches a headset to my scalp and tapes wires to me forehead. That's all, he says, and promises it won't hurt.

The screen comes alive and I watch green lines speed across from right to left, rising and falling in waves, while Anders adjusts the dials. Try not to think about anything, he says, let your thoughts float. I close my eyes and allow the fading warmth of the pot lull me. An old dream returns, but now I'm awake, aware of it, watching it as I listen to Anders fuss with his machine. The water is dark and I am swimming, swimming forward deep inside it, the sea or ocean, while ahead I see a shape, a ship perhaps or a figure, a hand reaching out, which I try to grab. The image shatters, literally cracking into a thousand pieces when Anders shakes me by the shoulders. I open my eyes and find his face almost pressed into mine. I'm sure only seconds passed, but Anders says I've been asleep for more than an hour. He's grinning. The data he recorded is excellent, some of the best yet.

7

Basam is on the terrace lifting weights. The barsati door is open and sends a cone of light across the concrete. Basam grunts at me, a nighttime greeting, as I take one of the plastic chairs and set it up near the edge. I look down into the narrow canyon of the alley. A few lights throw pools onto the cobblestoned and pot-holed roadway while a couple of figures, wrapped thickly in shawls, move cautiously amid the shadows. Low-powered motorbikes gurgle and dogs nose through garbage and a cow sleeps, blocking the centre of the road. A car attempts to edge around it for two long minutes, trying both sides of the cow, until finally the driver surrenders to the situation and reverses down the block. Basam drops the weight bar heavily onto the roof, sending a shiver through my feet.

Eh, he says, pulling up the other chair and joining my vigil, so what motherfucker did you fuck tonight? I ignore him and make a motion to stand, but he takes hold of my wrist and keeps me seated. Don't be so fucking sensitive, man, he says, a dick in the ass and it's still ass, who gives a shit that ass has a dick or not. I tell him to go fuck himself and he laughs, Yeah, baby, the dream. He wraps an arm around my neck and pulls me close and picks up his phone and navigates to a website. He smells of the street, of age and heartbreak and corruption, as if its very essence has found a home inside him. Look at this, he says, beginning to scroll through as he holds the screen up for me to watch. It's endless shots of dicks pounding asses, one after the other. That's it, he says, that's all it is, and laughs. He pauses on a few, wanting me to admire them with him. I push him and the phone away and stand and retreat towards the door and he calls out to me, Remember the shawl, man, and the shirts. He presses his arms to his chest, pretending to shiver, I gotta look good if I wanna pound some bitches. I walk inside and before I close the door I catch a glimpse of him, hunched over his phone, his chest and face lit by the screen, scrolling furiously through the short clips. He looks strangely like a child.

Jaggi is asleep and I do something I almost never do, or never allow myself to do, because I want to do it every night. I climb up to his bunk and let him wrap an arm around me and flood me with his sweat. Anders disappears, Basam disappears, so does the city, and all I am is a body wrapped in the arms of the man I love. Jaggi's odour on the sheets is a protective cloak and I fall asleep inhaling the aching musk of his taut body. I wake to soft orange light painting the walls and Jaggi gone to wherever he goes and I climb down to my own bunk. Basam watches me with a single open eye. He shuts it when I look at him. I pull the sheet tight over me and pretend to sleep.

8

A diploma hangs on the wall behind the desk, from Syracuse University in New York, trapped inside an ornate, silver-flecked frame. I can't tell if it's real or fake, but the subject,

Civil Engineering, written in obviously overly bold italics, and the bright orange and prominent honours ribbon, makes me question. The only other wall decoration is a large framed photograph of the Golden Temple, glowing in the night like some monstrous syrup-drowned sundae. I've been deposited here by a lackey, who simply told me to sit and wait, but I walk through the room like I own it. There are photos of his children, three girls, and his wife, and also his mother, and a small white dog, all sitting on his desk, which is neat, everything precisely arranged. A few papers, a pen, a landline telephone, various trinkets on a shelf behind him. A window looks out onto an airshaft, opening like an entrance to an underworld. The air conditioner's cracked housing is yellowed by age.

Mr Harbans Singh enters and greets me with a strong handshake and pulls me towards him, close enough that I smell his aftershave. He's dressed casually, in a brown checkered sports jacket and red tracksuit pants with white stripes running down each leg. Take a look, he says, still tightly gripping my hand and pulling me against his belly, the size of which shields his crotch. He indicates the bookcase which up to now I've ignored. It houses rows of near identical green hardbound volumes, all different thicknesses, some sort of great books of the world series. Pick one, he says, take it with you if you like. A quick glance across the titles shows me I know most, have read more than half. I pull one out, because it's slim and fits easily into my pocket. He asks how I learned to read so well, and I tell him, The nuns, just that, the nuns, and elaborate only after he presses me. At the orphanage, I say, one nun in particular, the others didn't take an interest, Sister Nirmal, who sat with me patiently, letter by letter, word by word, until I read my first book. What book was that? he says, and I glance across to the shelf and pick out the first book I see. *Robinson Crusoe*, I say. I'm already exhausted by his questions. Who does he think he is that he needs to know my story before he fucks me? The lying is equally dull, but telling the truth would only invite more questions, too many and too pointed. Besides, every time I say the word orphanage my tip always increases just that little bit. He pulls the copy of *Crusoe* from the shelf and hands it to me. Go on, he says, read for me. I turn to a page at random and there is Friday, mute and servile. I read a couple of paragraphs, confidently but at times haltingly, tripping deliberately over a few words, pretending I'm not as good a reader as I am.

When I finish, he brings his hands together in slow applause and invites me to sit. The door opens and tea and biscuits arrive, carried by the same lackey who showed me to this room. He offers me a cigarette but I decline. I want to get the business done and be out of here, and wonder why he's not asked me yet to walk around the desk and get on my knees. The scene is already tedious and then it gets worse. He starts to talk. I hate talkers, the ones who want to tell you their life story as if it justifies sticking their dick in your mouth or yours in their ass. The story is the usual. Partition. India. Pakistan. Death and refugees. His father this, his mother that. Poverty. Children. Bootstraps. Success. Blah blah it goes on. I check out and watch a fly buzzing in circles over our heads and wonder at the hubris of men like this, stealing my time to gratify their engorged and pathetic egos.

He surprises me by cutting short the litany of family tragedy and subsequent triumph and jumps to his feet and tells me to follow him. You're going to be working for me, he says. This is news to me. He wraps an arm tightly around my shoulders and leads me back out along the hallway. Don't look so worried, he says, you're with family now. He adds, Or do you want me to tell the police who the thief was who stole my sister's purse at her own father's funeral? He slaps me on the back, Only four hours, in the evenings, from ten to two, Monday to Friday! He's sure I can fit that into my busy schedule. His joviality unnerves me and there's a hint of mockery in that last comment. It would have been much easier just to suck him off and be gone. He releases me and we enter a large, open-plan office, with maybe twenty desks and a dozen people, all seemingly on the phone, chattering away, everyone speaking English. The windows are covered in silver foil and a row of fluorescent lights hang limp from the ceiling, casting the room into deathly relief. Everything is drained of colour, barely clinging onto life. Even the file cabinets look as if they're on the verge of collapse. It could be two in the morning or two in the afternoon. No one would know the difference.

The workers are all men, except for a single woman, in her twenties, who strides towards us as we enter. She's dressed smartly, in a salwar kameez and chunni, which hangs loosely over her shoulders. This is him, she says not as a question and not looking at me. Mr Harbans Singh nods. He is leaving me in capable hands, he tells me, and repeats that last phrase, capable hands, as if it means something between the two of them. Before he walks away, he studies me again, the way he did at the gurdwara, evaluating me with that lip-curling look of repulsion. I have the same vision, of him fucking me from behind and bursting into tears, but I push it aside and turn to my new guide through this Karol Bagh hellscape, and ask if her name is Beatrice, Dante's beloved guide, not through hell but through heaven. The pompous reference flies over her head, and she says, We have no names here, not our names at least. She grabs a manila envelope and tells me to follow her.

9

My new name, she tells me, is Special Agent Bob Masters from Washington, D.C., a member of an F.B.I. task force investigating potential tax fraud among the elderly in the United States of America. She says again, potential, and advises me, remember that, always say potential, as nothing, obviously, is proved yet. This is America, she says, and in America, you are innocent until proven guilty, even in cases of tax fraud. She leads me down the stairs and we step into Delhi's choking air, a million miles from any idea of America and its notions of guilt and innocence.

A nearby industrial compressor blasts out heat and noise and she offers me a cigarette and lights one for herself. Those people, she says with a nod of the head, indicating the room we just left, are the day shift, totally legit, actual fucking call centre shits who think that's what this place is. She sneers when she says this. Not the brightest, but they speak English, and that's what we need most of the time. Anyhow, she adds, they provide cover. She takes a long drag of her cigarette and blows the smoke directly into my face and smiles when I don't so much as flinch. You'll meet everyone tonight, she says, but in the meantime study these pages, it's all you'll need really. She hands me the envelope and I pull out several sheets. It's a series of scripts for mock conversations between someone called Agent and someone called Potential Fraudster. The different pages offer different scenarios, but the opening is always the same. You been doing this a long time? I ask, and she rolls her eyes and drops the cigarette at her feet and stubs it out. This isn't a fucking date, she says, and tells me to arrive fifteen minutes early, So we can set you up. She turns and disappears back inside the building.

The door slams behind her and I hail an auto-rickshaw to Paharganj and get out at the opening of the Main Bazaar. I weave my way through listless cows and SUVs and trash and bhang-stoned backpackers and reach one of the tourist cafes that sits high up, overlooking the street action below. It's quiet this time of day, only a dreadlocked couple staring into phones, and a woman, maybe an American, reading a book and drinking herbal tea. Below is a crowd of stalled traffic and blasting horns, while a cow sits unconcerned in the heart of the intersection. A policeman wanders, casually striking beggars across the back with a lathi.

I ignore the envelope Beatrice, or whatever her name is, gave me and pull out the book I took from the office and start reading. Someone's mother is dead but the narrator doesn't seem to care, about that or anything else. I've read it before but I've forgotten everything. The waiter arrives, smartly dressed, his clothes ironed and starched. I order a lassi but he hesitates and holds his pen over the pad. I can see the question in his eyes. Should I take this order or should I tell this goonda to get lost? I rest my hand on the book, the book obviously in English, and he takes my order. After he leaves I take a quick look around. I'd noticed the shawl when I walked in, packed in clear plastic and sitting next to the female backpacker, crisp and newly purchased. Both are still buried in their phones.

The American's purse, poking out from her backpack, is in ridiculously easy reach. I doubt I'll take either, not in a place like this where it's too easy to be stopped on the stairs, but I enjoy making a mental map of possibilities. It keeps me sharp.

10

What's the book? the American says. I'm halfway through the lassi when she calls out. I raise it and show her the cover and she says she read it in school. They let you read books like this in school? I ask, and she nods, and says she read worse at home, by worse, she adds, meaning more fucked up. Her parents are professors and they had all sorts of books at home, books certainly a kid shouldn't be reading, but neither of them ever took much notice of what she got up to, being ex-hippies and that shit with way too much money now, drowning in their fucking 401 kays and whatever. I don't know what she means, and think maybe 401 kays are a kind of jeans, but don't ask. I was a wild child, she adds, all the way out there in the heart of the suburbs. I tell her I think the book is pretty dumb and she says, yeah, she thought so too. She tells me the guy kills an Arab for no reason and then everyone turns on him. There's a name for that kind of book, she says, she means in philosophy, but she can't remember. Actually, she says, talking almost nonstop at this point, she remembers nothing about the book at all, just that he kills the Arab, and sometimes thinks maybe she's not so bright, she's read a lot of books but can't remember much of anything she's ever read, not even the titles of the books. She stands, lifting her teacup, and says, May I? indicating the seat next to mine. I nod and she walks over. She's dressed in a cheap salwar kameez and sandals, the kind you buy in any of the tourist traps along the Bazaar. Her dark hair is tied back in a long braid. When she joins me, the waiter looks at both of us with suspicion.

Her name is Susan, she says, and I tell her mine, and then she says, in Hindi, My name is Susan, and she tells me she's learning the language. She says more, stuttering over her words, but getting the grammar right. I tell her her Hindi is good and she says, No, it's terrible, but one day maybe. She's been living at an ashram in the north, in the hills in Himachal. She'll go back soon, if it gets too hot in Delhi, she loves the light, the beauty, the birds in the morning, the mist on the trees. Have you been there? she asks, and I say no, I've never left Delhi, and she says, suddenly, with her American willfulness, We must go together, the two of us, we must travel to the hills, how can you live in India and not see the hills? We talk about the ashram, her guru and what he teaches, and I tell her about Jaggi's dream, I call him my friend, of going to live on the beaches of Goa or Kerala. She's travelled to

Kerala, and Goa, and farther south, and even as far east as Assam, and I think of this American who knows so much more of this country than I do, than I probably ever will. She points to the envelope, and asks what's in there. Take a look, I say, pushing it across the table towards her. I explain it's for my new job, that I'm starting tonight. I'm supposed to have read these but I haven't even looked at them, I say.

I watch her face as she reads and her confusion turns to a kind of glee, or thrill. You're one of those guys, she says, and I say, I'm going to be. Her mom gets these calls, she just hangs up, but when her dad answers he gets angry, he starts arguing with the person, asking them if it makes them feel good stealing from old women, from people who could be their mothers or grandmothers. I tell her to keep her voice down, and she lowers it, and I say I don't have a mother or grandmother, or sister or anything, and I don't know how I'll feel because I haven't started yet. Her guru says there is no such thing as good or evil, or right action or wrong action, there is only action, and reaction, and no matter what you do, and you can do anything, from helping a starving man to killing a child, it cannot be called right or wrong, or good or evil, it can only be called action, and reaction.

She leans against me, flooding me with the scent of her skin and freshly shampooed hair, pressing her body into mine and bringing her lips right up to my ear, so I feel them as she whispers, I think it's so cool, I think it's incredible, to just do something, no matter what it does to others, to just act in the world. Her breasts push against my arm and then she pulls back. She insists we meet again tomorrow, right here, because she wants to hear all about it. There's a glow of almost feral excitement in her eyes, and I can't decide if I should admire her or pity her.

I pay the bill, and say I'll meet her, but ask a favor. It requires some acting, I say. The excitement returns to her eyes, Is it kinda fucked up? she whispers dramatically, and I nod, and explain I want her to make a small scene, not a big one, like maybe she's seen a cockroach or something, and to do it just when I'm walking past the backpackers. She nods seriously, and I take my book and stand to leave and walk towards the stairs. I don't need the scene, I could take the shawl without it, but something in her eyes makes me ask her. People like you more, they're more invested, if you include them, even in petty crimes like this. I don't know yet how I'll profit from her, but know I can if I keep her hanging around long enough. There's always money to be made from an American, especially a woman. An American woman on your arm opens almost any door.

On cue I hear her voice cry out and I quickly reach down and grab the shawl and calmly walk on, pausing only for a second at the top of the stairs. That's when I notice the waiter. He's looking directly at me with a mixture of contempt and amusement, as if he is telling himself how right he was all along. It was her cry that alerted him, I'm sure, otherwise I would have just disappeared, evaporated like a spirit. I hurry down three flights, push past the surprised doorman, and throw myself back into the city's crushing din.

11

Basam is lying on his bunk, once more staring into his phone. I walk in and take the shawl, still wrapped in its protective plastic, and throw it at him. He sits up and looks at me, irritated, and grabs the package and immediately throws it back. It lands at my feet and he says, Give it properly, not like some asshole. I make a show of picking the package up and walking the few paces between our beds and bowing and handing him the package. He's unfazed by the theatricality, as if he's auditioning for his future role as a pasha with his own kingdom. He rips the plastic off and discards it on the floor and unfurls the shawl across his legs. He tests the fabric between his fingers and stands and wraps himself tightly in it, then sits down, ignoring me as he does all this, looking suddenly like an old man, hunched over. I can see him sitting next to an oil drum in the night, a fire burning inside it, in the cold of winter, his breath pooling in clouds as he rubs his hands for warmth and guards the homes of people so rich they could buy him a thousand shawls and not notice the impact on their wallets.

After a minute, he nods, and looks at me. Okay, he says, and stands and walks across to where I'm sitting. One day, he says, pushing his crotch towards my face. One day what? I say, and he looks down at me and says nothing for a minute, then repeats that phrase, One day, and pushes his crotch closer to my face and pumps it a couple of times back and forth. He retreats to his bunk and flops down and returns to scrolling through his phone, as if I'm not there. The faint slap of flesh against flesh squeaks tinnily from the speaker while he stares, stony and unmoved. I know what he means. One day his patience will run out, one day he'll decide to fuck me, literally or figuratively or both. The reason he tolerates Jaggi is that I steal for him. I'm surprised we've lasted this long. Our bargain was that after three or four months of my stealing for him and the both of us paying his share of the rent, he'd disappear and sign the lease over to us. It's been six months and counting and there's little sign, other than this so-called Gurgaon gig, which I'm pretty sure is imaginary, that he's going anywhere. It's the reason Jaggi started pissing on the floor. To give Basam an extra push. Disappearing to the south looks better every day. Sometimes I wonder why we just don't do it, pack our few belongings and vanish into the sun-flooded anonymity of a beach. Everyone's patience is running thin. I can almost taste an explosion in the air.

12

The information appears on my screen like this: Mrs Elaine Drummond. Age 73. Widow. Former occupation: Homemaker. Residence: 28492 Sycamore Pass Road, Boise, Idaho. It's all there, recent bank balances, pension and other retirement accounts, available credit, etc. I see one line which reads 401(k) balance and laugh at it. So that's what it means. Mrs Drummond's phone rings automatically when I use the mouse to click a green button on the screen. If a female voice answers, which it does, I say, Mrs Drummond, Mrs Elaine Drummond? I listen to her cautious yes, and add, Of 28492 Sycamore Pass Road, Boise, Idaho? I hear another cautious, extended, Yes, followed by, That would be me, who is this speaking please? I tell her I am Special Agent Bob Masters, that I am calling from Washington, D.C., and that I'm a senior investigator assigned to a task force specialising in cases of potential tax and wire fraud. I tell her not to be concerned, this call is routine, she is not in any trouble, nor is anyone she knows in any trouble as far as we know, it's just that her name was red-flagged during a routine records check and we discovered her account had potentially been compromised. My voice is digitally enhanced by a computer program called YankIFY. It makes me sound like an American. I repeat, Did you hear that, ma'am, your account was red-flagged and that's why I'm calling because there seems to be a case of potential fraud that might be associated with it. My account, she says, what account are you talking about?

I tell her again not to be alarmed, there is absolutely no issue of her being involved in any fraud whatsoever, it's just that these things happen from time to time, very rarely if I'm honest, and it's honest, hardworking Americans like herself that have to deal with the inconvenience of it. Again, son, she says, what account are you referring to? I apologise and say, of course, your IRS account, I mean your tax account at the Internal Revenue Service, it seems there has been some fraud, I mean potential fraud, detected there, and we're simply initiating an investigation. She knows nothing about an IRS account, or a tax account, has no idea she has one, and I tell her all Americans have one, at least all Americans who file taxes, or at least pay them, or have paid them in the past, it's really a formality, it's where her taxes are deposited, it allows the Federal Government to track each tax payer's contributions, and as I understand it, few tax payers even know they have such an account, there's no reason for her to know about it. We talk like this for a while, with me explaining the intricacies of her tax account, and she expressing increasing surprise at the very existence of it.

Finally, I get to the point. There is a discrepancy with your account, and while we investigate any areas of potential fraud, I need to warn you that you may be in jeopardy not with us but with the IRS. There is a small deficit in your account of four thousand three hundred and sixty-eight dollars and seventy-three cents. This is money that is missing from the United States Treasury, and in one way or another it needs to be replaced. I can assure you it will be replaced at the conclusion of our investigation. The problem is that in the meantime you may be subject to an IRS enforcement process which may require your appearance at a tax court here in Washington, D.C. In very rare cases this includes the imposition of a fine or even brief imprisonment at a federal facility. Imprisonment, she says, for what exactly? For having a discrepancy in your tax accounts, I explain, I mean a serious discrepancy, anything larger than one thousand dollars. For sums smaller than that the enforcement process is entirely different, much more human, or humane, if you don't mind my saying. And this all happens in Washington, D.C.? she says, and I say, Yes, ma'am, it does, right here in the capital of our great nation, you may be asked to come here to straighten it out. That's a long way from Boise, I add. It surely is, she says, it's a helluva long way, pardon my French, and she asks how possible such an enforcement action might be, and adds, I'm an old card room hustler, honey, so tell me straight, what are the odds? I genuinely don't know, I tell her, I've seen it go so many ways, it depends on the officer you get, and I guess what kind of day he's having, and I add, excuse me, what kind of day *they're* having, we can't assume anymore, can we, I mean how they, how do I say it, identify. She laughs at that, a serious, lifelong smoker's laugh, It's a funny world, she says, sure has become one, don't know a man from a woman no more, and adds, yup, those damn pencil pushing Poindexters they have up there in Washington, don't they know there's regular folk out here. I agree, I tell her, I totally agree, honest Americans, ma'am, like you and me, just doing their jobs. Is there anything I can do, she asks, to make sure something like this doesn't happen?

We've travelled a long way, Mrs Drummond and I, through the woods in the night and now we're close to the city in the dark, the undiscovered country, glowing distantly, as we struggle forward, and I'm ready, with luck, to show her that shining destination. As we talk, the room gradually grows quieter around me. One after another, my colleagues remove their headsets, cut short their phone calls, and rise from their chairs to gather and listen. Even Mr Harbans Singh appears, and stands staring down, leaning over the partition, Beatrice to his right. Everyone is enraptured, and except for me, there is silence in the room.

There is something, I tell her, something that will prevent the IRS from initiating any kind of enforcement action against her, and it's quite simple. She needs to deposit the exact amount of the deficit to be held in escrow at a dedicated bank account we have here at the FBI for exactly such contingencies. We'll inform the IRS we have the money deposited pending the outcome of our investigation, at which point, no matter what happens, the money will be returned. There's no need to worry, I assure, we'll send you a receipt along with a promissory note explaining in detail that these are your hard-earned funds and belong to no one else, least of all the United States Treasury, and that all that can be done with them is that they are ultimately returned to no one else other than the depositor, meaning you. Everyone knows you had nothing to do with this potential fraud, but this is government, and if some pencilneck sees the books are not balanced no one knows what might happen, you understand. Let's call it acting out of an abundance of caution. And I should add, you can have access to this money at any time with a simple phone call. We'll transfer back whatever funds you want within five business days, at the maximum. We've done this thousands of times, maybe hundreds of thousands, the money is always returned, one hundred percent of the time, with interest accrued. The interest, by the way, is tax free. It's a formality in every sense of that word. Because I'll tell you what happens at the end. Either we recover any or all of the monies stolen in the potential fraud or we inform the IRS that it is not potential fraud, but definitive fraud, the kind of fraud that can be no one else's fault but their own. That's always the kicker, ma'am, because no one wants to look at their own errors, their own failures, their own character flaws. It always ends exactly the same way. The case is closed and your money is returned. We can make the transfer right now if you like. I can assure you, it will help put your mind at ease.

Mrs Drummond vacillates, considering her options, worrying about all that money, and asks several times, You're sure I can have access to the money whenever I like, and says she must talk it over with her son first, that she needs his advice, she's not comfortable taking such an action on her own. I tell her that's fine, in fact I think it's the best course of action, and offer her my personal number where she can contact me at any time, day or night, if she decides to go ahead with the process or has further questions. I encourage her to have her son call me too, but to make sure she's there when he does. I'll need her spoken authorisation to discuss her case with anyone else, even immediate family. Just don't wait too long, I say, and before I hang up I ask, How's the trout on the Snake River this spring? and she says, Oh, good, real good, better than usual I think, my youngest caught a ten pounder not two weekends ago, and then says, You know, son, why not, why not let's just do this, no reason to worry my eldest over it, he's got a lot on his mind with a new baby, my fifth grandson, and adds, Will this be complicated?

As I'm processing the payment, I tell her I've been taking a closer look at her account, and that sum is not the only red flag for me. I've seen this many times, I say, there's a specific deficit, like the one she has, but there are signs of ongoing potential activity, I mean fraudulent activity, and if I were her, if I truly wanted to guarantee there is no trouble from the IRS I think I'd act proactively and raise the amount of the deposit to maybe ten thousand. Call it an insurance policy, I say, and add, When it comes to the IRS, being proactive never hurts. Of course, I say, we can do this later, that's no problem, it just depends on whether we catch it before the IRS flags it themselves, and that's assuming there even is more activity, which is no certainty. In my business, I tell her, nothing is certain.

13

I use the mouse to move the arrow across the screen to the red button to end the phone call and I'm greeted with applause and shouts of shabash and bravo. After almost an hour, I have raised the sum Mrs Elaine Drummond, of 28492 Sycamore Pass Road, Boise, Idaho, deposited into what she believed was her secure FBI escrow account to twenty-five thousand dollars. Mr Harbans Singh has never seen anything like it. He calls it an extraordinary performance. I should be on the stage, he says, in the movies, I'm a born con artist! He pulls me from my chair and slaps me on the back, as do many of the others. In one phone call, I've made more than the whole room has ever made in a single night.

Beatrice eyes me coolly with admiration. I liked how you did that, she says, you had her wrapped around your finger from the very beginning. It's the first time she's ever complimented me. It's how you introduce yourself, how you start, I say, it sets the tone, the level of trust, in the end it's all about trust, I mean her trusting my voice. It's a spell, I add, but we both take part in casting it, if you understand me. The Big Man, she says, wants you to teach us how you do it, offer tips, lessons. I shrug, sure, and accept a cigarette. I smell her perfume, it's earthy, lively. Usually we don't smoke in the room. No one likes the sound of someone coughing on the other end of a phone line. For my triumph they've bent the rules.

I had doubts about you, she says, when he brought you in, I thought it was a mistake. Guys like you, she says, and I ask, Guys like me? You know what I mean, she says, but you're not like other whores, not the ones he picks up. I dunno, I say, I don't know what other whores are like. She looks at me evenly, as if trying to uncover some secret scored deep into my face, into the skin itself. Cheap, she says finally, blowing smoke into the air, he likes them cheap. After the excitement dies down, she tells me the Big Man wants to see me in his office.

Mr Harbans Singh pours me a whisky, filling the glass near to the top with water, and tells me to take a seat. When I was watching you, he says, and you had her at five thousand, what's her name, oh yes, Mrs Elaine Drummond, of Boise, Idaho, a name that will go down in history, well, when you had her at five thousand I couldn't believe my ears, he's going to get her for that much, I thought, and then you fucked it up, you really fucked it in the arse, you got cocky, you were going to lose everything when you pushed for ten. I was sure she was going to hang up. Ten thousand, no one's ever got anywhere near that, and I wanted to scream, stop, please stop, but you kept going, and when you suggested, just in case, she might want to deposit twenty-five thousand I almost had a heart attack. Incredible, he exclaims and claps his hands, after two weeks of being here, you tear up everything we've been doing for a year and show us a whole new path. He laughs and takes a long drink and pours more for both of us from the decanter sitting on the desk. Twenty-five thousand, in one phone call, he rhapsodizes, still unsure if he can believe it. You'll get a bonus for this, a big one. He leans forward and clinks his glass against mine.

Now come here, he says. I recognise the look in his eyes, the meaning of the curl of his lip. I stand and walk around the desk, certain of what's coming next. He looks me up and down, then runs a hand across my belly while his other hand reaches around and finds my ass, which he caresses gently. He spreads his legs and pulls me forward and takes hold of my thighs and squeezes them and presses his face into my crotch and pulls back and he lets his fingers play across the zipper on my jeans. Such a handsome boy, he says, such a talented boy. I drink whisky and lay the glass down and touch the top of his head. His hair is mostly gone but his skin is still soft. You're all mine, he says. He undoes my belt and unbuttons and unzips my jeans and pulls my underwear down and takes my penis out and admires it, fingering it along with my balls. I'm limp but gradually I grow hard as he runs a tongue along the tip. He wraps his mouth around my cock and starts to suck and I find the decanter and refill my glass, ignoring the water this time.

As I'm drinking, Beatrice walks in without knocking. She is carrying a folder and takes in the scene without so much as a flinch. The same with Mr Harbans Singh, who continues sucking me off as if nothing else is happening. The final numbers for tonight, Beatrice says, laying the folder onto the desk. Beatrice pauses at the door on the way out, and says, Good night Big Man. She looks directly at me as she says it. I look at the photos on his desk. Wife, daughters, mother, little white dog, everyone smiling, even the dog, and I wonder at his life at home, Mr Harbans Singh, family man. Do they gather and watch television, do they go out to fancy restaurants, vacation at swank resorts, is he already planning marriages for his girls, searching for suitable boys?

I come in his mouth and he swallows and circles my hips with his arms and tightly hugs me. He presses his face into my crotch until my cock is pushed all the way down, deep inside him. I hear him gagging yet still feel his tongue searching for my balls. Finally, he releases me and shudders and lets out a long sigh. Immediately he opens a drawer and he produces a bottle of neon pink mouthwash and a neatly folded hand towel. He gargles with the mouthwash, tipping his head far back, and finds a decorated bronze cup on the shelf behind his head and spits the mouthwash into it, then spits onto my cock and thoroughly cleans it using the towel, polishing the head to a high sheen. He's careful to also wipe my balls, saying as he does this, Always remember, cleanliness is next to godliness, my father always said that. He repeats his promise that my bonus this week will be extra large and I pull my underwear and jeans up and buckle my belt. Looking down I see, in the corners of each eye, the slightest hint of a tear.

14

The session with Anders ends quickly. Just the rough sex, no tender lovemaking this time. There's time enough for him to roll out the machine again. The last time, he says, the results surprised him. He attaches the electrodes and starts talking in that way he sometimes does. He's mapping dreams, he says, he has teams travelling all across India, doing exactly what he's doing now, recording the dreams of ordinary people, people like me. He's building what he calls a dream map of the country, a kind of dream library.

Before I can ask why, or even what that is, he tells me to close my eyes and relax. He turns the machine on and I sit there like before, drifting into thoughts of Jaggi, and that old dream. I'm swimming, swimming forward through the dark. The sensation is liberating. My body dissolves into the water and soon I'm nothing but currents, an invisible body in the depths. When the session is over, he tells me he's leaving early the following morning and needs to prepare. Several of the bookshelves are stripped, and when I look at them quizzically he says not to worry, he needs the books, that he'll be back. The tip is extra large, three times the usual size. So you won't forget me, he says.

I have hours on my hands and decide to walk, as I often do, until the streets become my home. The night can wrap a person as easily as a shawl, or a body. The few times I've felt free, if I've ever felt it, it's these wanders through the city at night. It's what I was doing when Anders said he spotted me during our previous encounter. An hours-long walk through the darkness of Delhi. It lets me think, or better still, helps me not to think, instead to go blank like one of those gurus who live in mountain caves.

Every city is a day city and night city, and there's another one, hidden inside the night city, when a hush settles over the world and you can walk for hours along empty stretches of boulevard or highway, even in a city like Delhi. It's a kind of desert, you see nothing for miles and yet it feels like being at the centre of things, the heart of creation, the universe revolving around you. Then the spell's broken. Something unexpected catches your eye. Once a group of dancers, all men, all naked as I soon realised, their bodies white from ash, appeared as if out of nowhere. They hardly made a sound. All I could hear was the faint whisper of their feet shuffling across the blacktop. A dozen or more, and they looked in pain, or that's what I first thought, they must be sadhus or madmen escaped from somewhere. It was only when I drew close that I saw they were dancers. Their bodies writhed, but slowly, and their faces were fixed in different states of torment. I stopped and watched and fell under their spell until finally they moved on. I thought this must be what looking at a great painting feels like, but an alive painting, living and breathing somehow. They vanished as quickly as they appeared, swallowed by the night and fog.

The stillness of the air tonight reminds me of that night, and the dancers are on my mind as I move through the night's hidden city, when I hear footsteps breaking through into my reverie. I've passed the Delhi Golf Club and now the mansion walls of the rich rise on all sides. I slow my pace and the footsteps slow, then I walk quickly and they quicken. I can tell from the sound the shoes are too large, and assume they're stolen. I stop in a pool of lamplight and the footsteps go silent, then they return and begin approaching. A thin figure emerges out of the darkness. He is wearing a cheap jacket, which is also too large, and when he is standing next to me nods that I should keep walking, which I do with him beside me. I recognise him when I see him in the light. It's the waiter who watched me steal the shawl. His face is gaunt and his eyes wide. From the look of him I can tell he's stoned or drunk, or probably both. His day off, no doubt, which he confirms. It's my day off and I was visiting a friend, he says. I wonder what kind of friend he would have, here among the mansions of central Delhi, but don't push it. There's a faint scent of cologne sliding off his skin. Either a day old or someone else's. I recognise it but can't remember where from. I saw you as I was leaving, he says, I've been looking for you, brother.

I don't like how he says brother and say nothing, deciding to let him talk. Most people will hang themselves if you let them talk, and I figure he will too. But he doesn't talk, not at first, and we walk together in ever stiffening silence, until he pulls a hand from of his pocket and holds it out, palm open and up. That's it, I think, he just wants money, a late night shakedown. I grow angry and want to kick him and tell him to get lost. I stop myself when he speaks. She's waiting for you, he says, she's been waiting for you every day. The guru chick, he adds. Then with a sneer, Brother. He clasps and unclasps his open hand a few times, just in case I'm having trouble understanding. She's still there? I say, and he says, Yes, everyday. She wants you, brother, he says, I see it in her eyes, can smell how wet her pussy is. I say, If you're lying, and he shrugs,

Maybe she's there tomorrow, maybe not. I pull out one of the five hundred rupee notes Anders gave me and push it into his hand. He closes his fist around it and stuffs the money into his pocket, and then shows me that same hand again, palm up and open. Look, brother, he says, the hand's still empty.

This goes on a few more times, with me down a few more bills, and with him crooning into my ear, Think of all that wet pussy, bro, wet American pussy. I grow bored and form a fist and punch him hard in the belly. He crumples into a ball on the sidewalk. I can grab the money back but then I'd be banned from the café. Something about the American makes me want to see her again. The waiter clutches his stomach as he lies on the ground, eyes furious and scared. I'm not your bro, I spit at him, and turn and walk away. A guard wrapped in a shawl watches from across the street, sole spectator for this late-night show. A grin blossoms across his face. I reach the corner and see the waiter climbing to his feet, still groaning. I wave down an auto and give the driver an address. I don't want the waiter chasing me down the street. The driver sets off and the blast of cool air invigorates me. His hands are wrapped in old rags and a scarf tightly covers his face, so he looks like a movie mummy who only sees through the slit for his eyes. The streetlamps race and their lights glint like starbursts through the mist. I change my mind and give the driver another address. Because Anders finished early, I remember I still have time.

15

The auto struggles through the final few alleys while the packed, uneven mud of what's left of the roadway jolts my head against the roof bar. We come to a stop and the driver deposits me at the end of a lightless alley. When he drives away, his single, working headlight jitters madly across the half-built housefronts and soon I'm plunged into almost total darkness. I find the door I'm looking for and push through it into a hallway, also unlit except for light leaking from under another, farther doorway. I grope until I find the handle. The rumble of voices from inside beckons like an invitation and I step into a low-ceilinged room. The walls are painted a faded yellow and ornate velvet couches, all different colours, are scattered throughout. A far-too-large-for-this-room chandelier hangs so low everyone has to duck or strain their neck to pass it. Beyond is a low, black-painted stage, with a single microphone on a stand sitting abandoned. Music's playing. Mohammed Rafi and Asha Bhosle. Their voices spin through the air, making it dizzy, narcotic. Those old songs are like a time machine, and here we are, hurtling backwards into a destroyed past.

I know most here by sight, but hardly anyone by name. This is Jaggi's scene, not so much mine. A few heads nod towards me in welcome and someone hands me a bottle of whisky. I don't see who it is, but they must have noticed I broke one of the unspoken rules, one I almost always break, which is bring your own. I usually don't need it, as

Jaggi always has enough to spare. I take a drink and search for him. One of the queens eyes me up and down and says, You gonna drink all that? I shake my head and pass the bottle. She's in a miniskirt and sequined halter-top and her belly bulges over her belt. Your girl's in the back, she says. There's a whiff of moustache clinging to her upper lip and her bare legs are unshaven. I guessed, I say, and she takes a seat and pats the empty cushion next to her. You don't want to disturb her while she's preparing, she says, and I accept the offer and sit down. Her strong perfume cuts through the cigarette smoke. It's mostly queens tonight, a few gays, and a couple of the regular fag hags I've seen around. She presses up against me and lights a cigarette and offers it, then lights one for herself. We've talked before but I don't know her name. Once when I asked she said, Anything you want, so I started calling her that, Hey, Anything You Want, but she didn't get the joke. Every time I said it, she made a face like I was offering her something, something she clearly did not want. She's not the fastest train in the station. I'm happy to let her slide against me and chatter as I wait for Jaggi's set. She always has something to say.

She's in love, she tells me, and lays her head against my shoulder, a tea boy in Saket, at J Block Market, not a boy of course, but who knows how old he is, she has no idea about age, hers or anyone else's, and a tea boy's, how's she supposed to guess that? She lifts her head and takes a drink and hands the bottle back to me. As she turns, I see the faint outline of a bruise covering one side of her face, poorly masked by makeup. I don't ask about it. Another of the unspoken rules. I doubt there's a person here not hiding a bruise or three. They had a little make-out session, she and the tea boy, in the lobby of the building next to the watch store. She sighs thinking about it. They were interrupted by one of those damn aunties. She came charging at them with her umbrella. The boy just ran. Out the door and into the street. Poof, she says, gone like that. And now where is he, she asks, throwing her hands up. Do you think I made him lose his job? she wants to know. I shrug in response. The struggles of tea boys, amorous or otherwise, are not high on the ladder of my concerns. She talks on, telling me about his gorgeous tight ass, the way his lips curled around hers when they kissed, and I distract myself by watching the room. The club's owner, Madame Yoyo, threads herself among the bodies, dressed in a red silk kimono embroidered with a dragon and holding aloft a champagne bottle and flute. Each time she pauses to chat, she leans so far forward I'm afraid she's going to topple, takes a long sip, nods her head, and refills her glass. The kimono glitters in the reflected light. When she spots me, she moves in my direction. I can't say walk, as her legs are hidden and give the impression of gliding, maybe an inch or so above the ground.

Anything You Want is still talking, worrying if she'll ever see her tea boy again, when Madame Yoyo cuts her off. Not that tea boy still, she says, and turns to me, She's been talking about nothing but that bloody tea boy for a whole week. She sits down on the other side from Anything You Want and presses against me, so I'm crushed between the pair of them. Where have you been hiding? she says, We haven't seen your face in a long time. Around, I say, and she laughs, and tells me she thought maybe me and Jaggi were on the outs. It's true, I haven't seen Jaggi's set in weeks, but between the Big Man and Anders, I've hardly had a night free. I've heard him rehearsing on the terrace a few times, new songs mostly, only a couple of which I recognised. This boy, this boy, Madame Yoyo chants, and wraps an arm around my neck and kisses me on the cheek. She's a small woman with a broad, round face that's always smiling, Assamese or something, no one knows for sure, or what her real name is. Jaggi brought me here soon after we met, and at that first meeting, she turned to me and before greeting me took my face in both her hands and laughed, You told me he was an orphan, this boy is no orphan! Jaggi was unfazed. It's the story he tells, he said, and whose business is his story but his. She kept staring into my eyes, as if trying to uncover a secret, another history, a buried me, and I pulled away and insisted I was an orphan, she had no right to question it. The exchange left me angry. She'd seen through my lie, into some hidden chamber.

She releases me and nods towards the door. That one, she says, not hiding her scorn, indicating a dark-haired young woman who's just walked in, some Frenchie journalist, and though she promises she's not writing about the place, Madame Yoyo doesn't believe her. There's a reason we keep this place low key, she says, but do you think this woman cares, all these journos care about is their next byline, steal this world for themselves, make a big splash with their dumbass scoop! The room has filled up, the couches overflowing, figures perched on armrests and laps, walls crushed with bodies. Someone on stage waves to Madame Yoyo and the lights dim and a spotlight illuminates a far door. The music stops abruptly and she rises and holds her glass high and taps it against the bottle. Into the sudden silence, she calls for everyone to put their hands together and welcome our very own, the Magnificent Jaggi himself! She's sets the glass and bottle down and is still applauding when she takes her seat again. Music fills the room and the door inches open and a foot appears, then a hand floating through the air, a few curls of hair, the wisp of a chunni, and finally, there is Jaggi, *my* Jaggi, I think, not theirs, not hers, not anyone else's, wrapped head to toe in gold, a glittering golden sari. The spotlight makes him glow. I feel a rush of pride as the applause transforms into cheers. The music rises and he takes the microphone and holds it, letting the moment build. The whole room stretches forward, craning their necks as they wait. It's like a cloudburst when he sings, the tension breaks and all that drenching, refreshing rain that is his voice pours down onto us. I realise I've been holding my breath and let out a long sigh. Jaggi has a way, I knew it when I first met him, he can hold a stranger mesmerised, a whole room, no doubt a stadium full of strangers. Everyone is hooked. It's an old song, one of his standards, one of my favorites. Soon the room is singing along and I'm drifting into dreams, or fantasies, of the two of us, walking hand in hand along a Kerala beach.

16

A flash of surprise crosses the doorman's face as I push past him into the short hallway that leads to the stairs. In his confusion, he's forgotten to open the door, and leaps back, fumbling as he attempts to clear a path for me. It's too late. I'm already climbing and he watches in disappointment, or is it resentment, as I reach the landing and turn and disappear. The café is busy, humming with life. I chose the hour well, hoping Susan would be here earlier than she was before, and there she is, seated exactly where I met her the first time. She senses my presence, and the moment I step off the top stair and into the room she turns to look directly at me. Her face brightens into a broad smile. I also catch the waiter's eye. He is standing at the counter, staring at me as I progress among the busy tables, a scowl blossoming across his face. I ignore him. I've paid my entrance ticket and don't need his approval.

I knew you'd come, she says, I was sure of it. She hugs me and kisses me on the cheek. She called her guru who promised her she would see me again, he said he had seen it in a dream, our reunion. He's never wrong, so I wasn't worried, she says. Her voice is oddly pitched and anxious. I take a seat. There's something she wants to show me. It's today's newspaper. She's trembling with excitement. She says I was meant to come today, because she is leaving tomorrow, travelling back to the ashram, and if I didn't come today not only would her guru have been wrong, which is impossible, but I would not have seen this.

She unfurls the newspaper to a double-page centre spread, all colour, with maybe a dozen photos, each with captions underneath. It's about the ashram and the good work it does in the community and beyond. At the heart, across both pages, is a photo of her guru. A long, tangled beard, a warm smile, richly-hued saffron robes, and his arms outstretched, enfolding maybe a dozen girls, their ages anywhere from eight to fifteen, all wearing identical blue and white smocks for uniforms. They're orphans, the caption says, girls saved from a terrible fate. Other pictures show him with local politicians, teachers, various of his acolytes. There's one of him with Susan, his arm wrapped tightly around her shoulders, pressing her into his chest. Her face sparkles in his presence. She watches me closely as I scan the page, expectant, though I'm not sure what for, what it is she wants from me. He looks like a kind man, I say, not knowing what else to say, and she says, It's not kindness, no, not at all, there's not a kind bone in his body, that's the point, the whole point of his teaching. There's nothing gentle in the destruction of the soul, she says, only violence, violence and annihilation.

Before she says more, the waiter appears and stands over me, staring icily. What would you like, brother? he says in a slow drawl. I pull out a large note and say I'll pay for the lady, we need to go. He lets out a quick dismissive snort and takes the bill. When he brings the change he lets it drop note by note and coin by coin onto the table. I gather up the money and leave an insulting tip of a few paise. All the while he watches from the counter, looking every inch as if at any moment he might fly across the room and lunge at me. What's wrong with here? Susan says, failing to register the tension. Don't you smell it? I say, loudly in Hindi, so the tourists don't understand. Smell what? she says, replying in Hindi. Fear, I say as I take her hand and lead her towards the stairs. We walk down and push past the doorman, who checks me with his eyes. I take Susan by the hand and we navigate the pothole lakes and drowsing cows until we reach a stall on the far side of the intersection. What was all that about? she says, and I shrug, and then admit, Fallout from the shawl. She laughs, she forgot about that. She pulls me close, so that was why you never returned, I was wondering but didn't think anyone spotted you. It's over now, I say, I'll never see that asshole again.

We buy fresh jelabis and walk along the Bazaar to a food stall next to one of the old hotels, the Metropolis, and find our seats on a pair of weathered plastic stools. I order tea as Susan unwraps the sweets. They're hot and sticky, and she eats them greedily. Her fingers turn yellow and she holds them out for me to lick. Along with the sugar, I can taste the city on her, its smell and soot. The air is thick with the sound of car horns and tumult. She tells me she likes the waiter at the café, he's been nothing but sweet, and I say all he wants is to fuck her, and she says she knows and smiles and adds, Who wouldn't want to sleep with this? indicating her figure, taut and slender. She doesn't see anything wrong with what the waiter wants, let him want it. I'll probably fuck him next time I'm here, she says, and looks at me and says, Don't take it so hard, I'll fuck you if you want, tonight, why not? I didn't know I was taking it hard, or how I was taking it, but she must have seen something in my eyes, either that or she was playing with me. My guru says the body is a gift, she says, a gift from the universe, and who are we to claim that such a gift belongs to us and only us. Who knows who the gift belongs to, she says, it could be anyone, how dare we claim to know why this gift was given to us.

She talks about her body and about gifts and who owns what and who doesn't and what her guru says about all these things and others, then touches my arm and says she has a confession to make, a serious one. I watch her as I drink my tea, curious about what kind of confession she could possibly make. Just as she is about to speak, a beggar approaches. He's wearing little more than a loin cloth and the city's dirt and stands suspended over a twisted wooden stick and holds out a battered metal cup towards her, the obvious American. When she ignores him he brings the cup right up to her face and shakes it louder, demanding money. The few coins inside clang tinnily. She turns and grows angry, starts abusing him, Get out, she says, get the hell away, and the two argue for a few moments, until he steps back, his face sour and pinched. As he retreats, he looks over his shoulder and spits in our direction.

My guru, she says, says never give to these worthless types, he says charity blocks their spiritual journey, that in the end all you're doing is preventing them from achieving their destiny. She returns to her confession, and says what I showed her, the scripts in the envelope, and what I told her about my job, she told her guru. I can't lie to him, she says, I can't hold anything back. There are no secrets between a guru and his disciple, she says, there can't be, it's the one unbreakable rule. A single secret can destroy the whole relationship, it can cause a soul to lose the only thing it desires, freedom from the cycle of birth and death and rebirth. I'm not sorry, she says, but I thought you should know, so you don't tell me anything if you don't want to. I call him every night, she says, it's like confession, I tell him everything, he says I'm a special case, *his* special case, that it's rare to meet a soul so close to breaking free from of the cycle of life and death, birth and rebirth, he thinks I'm this close. She holds up two fingers and brings them together until they're almost touching. A hair's breadth, she says, but even a hair's breadth can be a year or a thousand years or a million he says, that no one knows how long it takes for a soul to travel even the tiniest distance. There are entire universes inside an atom, she says, so think of how many universes exist inside a single hair, more than stars in the sky, and that's just one human hair. Her eyes widen at the thought, and she looks at me, wildly, as if she is seeing some other man, some other being, or through me to a vision of eternity.

She grabs my hand, He wants to meet you, she tells me urgently, you must meet him, maybe he'll see that you're also a special case, that you're on the edge of extinguishing your soul. She is sure I am, she is sure that's the case, why else are we drawn to each other like this. Her grip tightens and she makes me promise, promise I will come and meet him, her guru, that I must meet him, the fate of my soul depends on it, she says breathlessly, and finally I agree, I make a solemn pledge. She closes her eyes and suddenly, for no reason I can see, begins to sob, her body trembling, then throws her arms around my neck. I'm so happy, she cries, I'm so, so happy! Her chest throbs against mine. She pulls away and wipes the tears and looks at her phone. It's almost time, she has to go.

She calls him everyday at six pm precisely. If she's thirty seconds late he will refuse her call, but more than that, he will refuse it again every day for five whole days.

60

Night in Delhi

It happened once, it'll never happen again. She'd never experienced anything like it, it was hell, literally hell, like being lost in the desert without water, thinking any moment the sun will kill you, praying for it to kill you. Every night she cried herself to sleep, and when finally, on the sixth day, he answered the phone, something extraordinary happened. The moment she heard his voice she flew out of her body, it was as if she was shot out of it, like a bullet from a gun, soaring through the air. She could see herself, in the room, holding the phone to her ear, talking to him, but she was no longer there, she was shooting higher and higher. In seconds she was outside the room, above it, above the hotel, the street, and kept rising, until she could see the city, on she went, up and up, into the smog and clouds, to the edge of space itself. The planet below her, the whole planet, it was hers, and she the god of it.

That's the kind of man he is, she says, the kind of gifts he gives people. Something in the way she speaks, her enthusiasm, her absolute certainty, it makes me want to slap her, to knock her down and give her a good kick, maybe in the head. I'm angry at having to sit here, angry at myself as much as her, listening to her nonsense, and for what, I don't know. Ten to one I'll get nothing out of her, that all this will be wasted labour. She makes me promise to meet her, later that day, after the call, and this time writes down my phone number. She never wants to lose me again. Seconds later, she is gone, lost among lurching SUVs and horn-blasting autos into the chaos of the Bazaar.

17

I walk to the cinema with its redbrick façade and strong smell of urine and years of red paan stains against the walls and buy a ticket and walk inside. I buy a samosa from the counter. There are cockroaches crawling on the cash register, small ones, and I ask for napkins and the clerk makes a whole long scene of searching for the box, picking it up and bringing it down in a cloud of dust, searching for a knife and using the knife to open the box, until finally, he produces a single tiny napkin and holds it out to me. I slap his hand away and grab a fistful and he looks at me, bored and outraged at the same time. It's hot in here, but when I walk into the theatre it's cooler but still muggy. Over the sound of gunshots on the screen the ancient air conditioner lets out its smoker's wheeze, trying, and ultimately failing, to cut the heaviness of the thick air.

The fight on screen is some Rambo thing, in a jungle with a shirtless man, muscled like a body builder and glistening in dirt and sweat. He's wearing a bandana and has bandoliers slung across his chest and carries a gun the size of a small tank barrel. He walks stealthily through a jungle, eyes searching in every direction, before suddenly stopping. The film goes into slow motion and the music rises dramatically as he raises the gun and starts firing. Bullets fly and flames burst from the barrel. Bodies of bad guys dance violently, writhing as their flesh is torn apart, and finally collapse. All the bad guys wear turbans, not Sikh turbans, not any kind of turbans really, just rolls of white cloth wrapped around their heads, raghead movie turbans. Each time one of them drops we watch the same scene repeated over and over, from different angles, their bodies spattered with blood. This goes on for several minutes and I eat the samosa and wipe my fingers and drop the napkins onto the floor.

In mid-shot, the scene changes. We're no longer in the jungle, but in some cheap hotel room, who knows where, the kind I know too well, with poor lighting and depressing wallpaper. A shaking camera records the action. A woman is being fucked hard in the ass while her mouth is getting fucked by another guy. Her clothes are torn and there are flecks of blood on her face, like she's been beaten right before the shot. The camera closes in to show the beginnings of a purple bruise around one eye as the dick pushes deep into the back of her throat. I don't know if it's real or fake, it's hard to tell anymore, I mean the rape, but my guess is it's real, some wannabe actress tricked into doing a screen test only to find her mouth stuffed with the director's cock.

Behind me I can hear boys snickering and laughing. I focus on the furniture, trying to figure out if I recognise the room, and therefore the hotel. It's easier than thinking about the woman and what happened to her. I've seen the bed before with its shiny half-moon shaped backboard, but the rest of the room is a mystery, I mean the sideboards and lights and wallpaper, and if it's the hotel I think it is, then there should be a door to a bathroom to the right but there isn't. We never see the faces of the two guys, just their dicks and sagging bellies. I'm surprised they can keep it up. The camera zooms in on the woman's face, showing tears, and I think I recognise her, that I've seen her around. I try and feel sorry for her but I can't. What was she thinking, answering some online ad for a casting call in a hotel room? I'm angry at her for falling for such an old trick. The snickering behind me stops and a strange kind of silence settles over the hall, it's almost mystical. All we hear is the sound of the air conditioner and the cries of the woman and the rapid, metronome-like slaps of the guys' flesh. I know the boys have their dicks out now, that they're living out their own sickening little gang bang in their heads.

The movie cuts again and the back rows erupt in cries of betrayal. We're in the mountains, everything is covered in snow, and music rises as a soldier, some officer type, dances on a snow-covered rooftop, singing to his love below of what else but his undying love. I'm glad the scene changed. I was getting sick of watching that woman. We all make bad choices, I guess, but not all of them end like that. There are a lot of cuts as the song goes on. We're in the forest and the two lovers peek at each other from behind trees or hold leaves up to hide their faces, like toddlers playing peekaboo. She sings she cannot love a soldier, because he'll die and then what will happen, and he sings but to love a dead soldier is to love a hero, a true Indian hero, a hero of the nation, what more could she ever want. They're on a high mountain lake in separate boats and then he's in a battle as she watches from a ridge. His comrades sing of the glory it is to love a dead Indian hero, how all her life she'll know her love died a true martyr of glorious India. One after another his comrades die from enemy fire, and only he remains, singing of his undying love and his glorious India.

A figure appears at the end of my row and makes slow progress along the seats until he cautiously settles down next to me. It's some old guy, in his sixties maybe, and for a minute we watch the song together, saying nothing, then he turns to me, Brother, he says softly, and his eyes flash down to my crotch. It's been a while since I've done anything in a cinema, but I'm not doing anything else so I shrug and name a price. Not too much, but not too little either. I want him to know I'm not just any cinema whore. He nods, accepting the price and unzips his pants and pulls his dick out and starts to stroke it. With his other hand he reaches over and unzips my pants and starts to finger my dick. In the light from the screen I see the flash of a wedding band on his hand. The lovers are in Venice now, jumping from gondola to gondola. Every girl's dream, I think, as the old man's dick begins to harden.

The scene changes again. We're in a mansion in the afternoon where plush couches form a semicircle. High, bright windows lead to a well-watered garden with statues and fountains visible. It's an orgy. Men sit on couches while women are on their laps, bouncing up and down as they get fucked. Huge, leafy potted plants dominate the room. The old man's hand tightens around my dick and he leans over and starts to suck me. The women all have their backs to the men, so they're facing the camera, their breasts jiggling as they jump up and down on the cocks. It all looks very strenuous. The camera pans across their bodies, and each time it lands on a new woman she makes a tortured, agonised expression. I watch the faces, bored, while the old man sucks me off and rubs himself. The camera pans to the lone flat-chested woman, and her face distorts instantly into a look of agony, or joy, I'm not sure which. That's not what interests me. I know the woman, for certain this time. It's Beatrice. She's younger, by maybe five years, but it's definitely her. The camera travels down her body to show her breasts and her pussy speared on a dick. There's a tattoo just above her pussy of a small butterfly. As her torso thrusts up and down the butterfly seems to flutter and almost fly.

The old man stiffens and comes. I'm glad I don't, because suddenly I want to get out of there. I pull his head free and he looks at me confused, as if thinking it's not over yet. I point to the come on his other hand and hold an open palm out for money. He picks a few of the used napkins off the floor and cleans himself, then drops them again, and pulls his underwear up and zips his trousers and ties his belt. I'm sorry, brother, he says, I have nothing, nothing at all. Only then do I get a good look at his face. The layers of sagging flesh, the defeat in his eyes, the years of failure spilling out in his loose and yellowed teeth.

A sudden fury takes me over. He thinks I'd do this for nothing, out of some twisted idea of charity. I grab his neck from behind and whisper, I could snap this right now. I dig my nails into him and he pleads, he's sorry, really sorry, he saw me and couldn't help himself, but truly, he has nothing, no money at all. I tighten my grip and with my other hand grab his arm. There is the wedding band, gold and glinting, and with my eyes I indicate this is what I'll take. A look of shock buries his face. No, please, no, he says. Tell her you lost it, I say. He looks at me again with those defeated eyes, She's dead, he says, this is all I have. Tears well in his eyes. He reminds me of the woman being raped, and I almost think maybe he did love her, his wife, that maybe I should leave him his wedding band, if that's what it is. I push any sympathy aside and begin to pull the ring from his finger. We struggle for it, both of us grabbing his hand and pulling it this way and that. It's clear from how difficult the ring is to prize free that's it's been on that finger for years, maybe decades.

The absurd battle continues but eventually I slide it off and pocket it but as I stand he jumps onto my back and hammers at me with his fists and we struggle again. It's mine, he cries, it's mine! I push him off and kick him to the floor. His head strikes an armrest on the way down. He looks up, horrified, his limbs flailing like an overturned insect. I walk out into the aisle. Beatrice is orgasming, or pretending to. Her face is in close-up, huge on the screen, and bizarrely twisted, as if this is a horror flick and she is watching a monster advancing towards her. When she comes she lets out a sickening cry, which explodes across the hall.

I remain standing watching while the old man gets to his feet and glares at me in fury, crying out, My wife, my wife! No one takes any notice, it's like he's screaming into a void, except then the kids in the back start laughing at him. One of them shouts in a high-pitched squeal, My wife, my wife. The others join in. He turns and raises his fist at them, but this just eggs them on. A couple of the boys stand and start pelting him with plastic drink bottles. The scene shifts again and I walk out to a final glimpse of the Rambo type blasting away at ragheads in the jungle. Behind him trees are all ablaze, as is a village, while a helicopter explodes in mid-air and begins to crash to the ground. The rising din of laughter from the back rows dies as the heavy swinging doors close behind me. In the street I feel the smog-choked evening sun on my skin and am surprised at the commotion, at all the people, who are they, where are they going, what are they doing? The old man's outraged face stays with me, but what did he expect, what was he thinking trying to cheat me. I finger the ring in my pocket and push past a beggar and plunge into the crowd and the noise.

18

When I get Susan's call I'm lying on the grass in the heart of Connaught Place, though it's hardly grass, only a few heat-blasted patches of some version of green survive. The rest is dead or dirt. Above me a giant Indian flag hangs limp in the dying rays of the sun and a layer of grey dust covers everything. She says she's close by and will be here in ten minutes. When she appears there's a huge grin on her face, and there's something different about her, about her eyes, the way she looks at me. Her gaze has a new intensity, if that's possible. She sits down next to me, almost formally, and takes my hand. He thinks you are, she says, he's not sure but he thinks you are. He thinks I am what? I ask, and she says, A special case, he thinks you are a special case. The guru will have to meet you before he makes a final diagnosis. That's the word she uses, diagnosis. He's been having dreams about you, she says. It was the same with her, before they even met the guru had dreams about her, though they'd only corresponded over email.

She takes my hands in hers and shuts her eyes and begins to breathe slowly, making a lot of noise as she does it. When I ask her if I'm supposed to be doing anything she gives a slight shake of her head. Bored, I watch my fellow citizens, sitting on this crappy so-called grass pretending it's a lawn, with their picnics and fine clothes. A breeze kicks up and plastic bags and ice-cream wrappers roll into the laps of women who flick the garbage away with practiced motions of the wrist. The men ignore the trash and let it pile up against their thighs. Susan opens her eyes and looks at me with the same intensity she had when she walked up. I felt it, she says, and I say too obviously, Felt what? and she says, The flames of the end of time brushing against your soul.

You're so close, she says, I know it for certain now, just a hair's breadth, and you will be free. She thinks I might be closer than she is. She lies down on the grass and I do the same and she takes my hand and we stare up at the enormous flag. It's a crime, she says, to ignore it, a crime against your soul, the only true crime anyone can commit, to ignore the imminent death of your soul. These moments happen, they're so rare, she goes on, so terribly rare, and if you miss it, you're thrown back into the void, into the cycle, into birth and death and death and birth, for centuries and centuries, maybe a million years, until the moment arrives again. She turns her head and looks at me. She says, I'm going to make sure that's not going to happen to you.

The evening breeze rises around us and lights go on one by one. Several spotlights illuminate the flag. It seems to glow, almost supernaturally. She talks on, in that way she does, about India, its greatness, the flag above us, why strength matters more than anything else, above truth itself, she says, because her guru says in the end truth is strength, truth is power, it's the only truth, it must be, because if a weak man meets a strong man, whose truth will survive, the strong man's of course, and it is the vital test of truth that truth always survives, no matter what comes against it. It is why a woman's truth is never truth, she says, because a man's truth is always stronger, man is action, her guru says, and woman is reaction, because you cannot have action without reaction, and you cannot have reaction without action.

I drift off and come back, and she is talking about how happy she is to have met me, that our meeting was destined, and I realise I can't take it anymore, the stream of idiocies flowing from her mouth. I sit up on an elbow and tell her she's full of shit, there is no destiny, there is no truth, her guru is a con man no different from me, that the only reason I stuck around was to see what I could take her for, but I'm bored now and she's leaving tomorrow so what's the point of keeping up the pretense.

I stand to leave but she takes my hand and holds me there. A night raag of car horns serenades the air while headlights circle us like predators and the sky forms a purple bruise slowly fading to black. She knows, she says, she's known from the beginning, that the only reason I was sticking around was because I was looking for an angle, some way to use her. She talked about it with her guru, who agreed, who knows too. You don't understand, she says, we are destined, that's all that matters.

I tell her about the old man at the cinema, how he tried to rob me after he sucked my dick, and how I stole the ring, the one thing he had left that reminded him of his dead wife, a wife he said he loved. She's not shocked, and I push her further. I tell her Jaggi's not my friend, he's my pimp, that he picked me up in a bar where I was working solo and threatened me unless I gave him a cut. See, she says without missing a beat, his strength became your truth. I laugh at her ability to twist anything. Her guru helps people like me, she insists, he's helped many, she means people who don't understand action can only go with reaction, never with action. Men are men, she says, women are women, they were made this way for a reason, it's one of the truths of the universe.

She asks to see the ring, and I hand it to her. She studies it in the lamplight. It glints in her fingers as she turns it this way and that. There's something here, she says, something written. She pulls out her phone and uses the flashlight to take a closer look. Her face grows solemn. See this, she says, showing me the ring in the phone's light, you were meant to steal this ring. The inscription is tiny, just two letters linked by an engraved heart, barely visible after years of being worn down on the old man's finger. The inside is so smooth it's hard to be certain what it says, but Susan knows, she has no doubts. The first letter is S, and the second is my first initial, both of us joined by that timeworn heart. She clutches my hand tightly and we hold the ring together. Her face glimmers in pale shades of orange and green from the flag's reflected light and tears form in her eyes. Do you understand now, she says, our souls are linked, they have been for eternity, and so will their deaths, this is a sign, our souls will perish together.

19

It's a slow night, no one's made anything, not one cent, including me. After an hour on the phone, I'm close to conjuring seven grand from Mrs Barbara Daniels in Des Moines, Iowa, who answers to Babs, widow of Mr Jackson Daniels and lifelong homemaker. Seven thousand dollars out of thin air. I've never heard of the place before I call her. I google it as we talk. Is Oktoberfest still going strong? I ask when she says she needs to speak to her son-in-law before sending me so much money. Oh it is, she says, I was there last year, but they're making changes, you know, and the crowds, it really is getting out of control, all those easterners moving here, looking for something real. I laugh at that, I might be doing that myself one day, I say. The line is slim, sketched so lightly, between fraud and its opposite, between evil and its twin, they look the same, wear the same clothes, one might as well be the other. For some reason, the old man I robbed of his wedding ring comes to mind. I can see him lying in the aisle, his arms and legs flailing, helpless and pathetic, and I think of the woman being raped on screen, how stupid she was for answering whatever ad it was she answered. Anger begins to bubble inside me, at myself, at the old man, at the woman on screen, and at Mrs Barbara fucking Daniels of Des Moines fucking Iowa. On hearing about Oktoberfest, Mrs Daniels' voice changes and she's taken over by the chummy Midwestern amiability I've come to recognise, to depend on, the need to connect, to think well of another person, to think there is no young man such as myself in this world. For some reason, it makes me hate her more. Well sheesh, she says, let's just do this, why don't we. If I was standing over her pointing a gun at her sleeping head, like the man in the book I took from the Big Man's office, I might as easily pull the trigger as not, that in the end it's the same thing.

I follow my script and try and raise the figure and her voice changes again. I decide I really want to push her. Something inside me wants to hurt this woman. Well, son, she says, let's keep it where we are for now, I'd feel more comfortable that way, and if the IRS comes after me, I guess, let the chips fall where they may. There's a clarity to her voice. She hasn't been drinking, at least not this early in the day. With most of my successes I always hear the slur of a morning drinker. I know it's time to pull back, to let the tension slack in the noose I have around her neck, to take what I can get. But I can't. I begin to push harder, to stress again the risks she's taking, to insist any money she gives me carries with it the full safety and guarantee of the United States Federal Government. Fifteen thousand, I suggest, fifteen thousand to help you sleep at night. Beatrice has appeared, her elbows perched over the partition, listening in on wireless headphones. She stares at me with rising alarm.

A ring of desperation enters my voice, its edge begins to fray. Beatrice runs a finger across her throat telling me to end the call, pocket the seven thousand and move on. I ignore her. Do you truly want to burden yourself and your family, I say, with the chance of being prosecuted by the IRS? Not just prosecuted, I add, *per*-secuted. I talk about the expense, the worry, tell her that such cases can drag on for years, years of lawyers, years of sleepless nights. My pitch rises, I know I'm losing her, I'm losing Babs Daniels of Des Moines, Iowa, and her hard-earned seven thousand dollars, dollars I could pluck right now, but something stops me. I don't care anymore and I can't stop. I want to take her for everything she has, ruin her if I can. I tell her she will be making the worst decision of her life if all she gives me is that lousy seven thousand, the one decision that she will look back on and say this was the day that wrecked her life, and the lives of her children and their families.

The room grows still, everyone stops talking and gathers around me. Beatrice screams silently, her mouth wide and wordless, Take the money! Babs, I say, can I call you Babs, and she says a quiet, Yes, and I say, Is this the legacy you want to leave your children, your grandchildren, years of litigation, years of not knowing when it's going to end, years of worrying about what might happen to you? There's a long silence on the phone, and finally she says, Yes son, I hear you, that is obviously not a legacy anyone would want to leave, but now I think about it, I think I will have to take your first offer and call you back after I've spoken to my son-in-law. She adds, He's in law enforcement, like yourself, so there's nothing to worry about there, if he thinks it's a good idea, and I'm certain he will, then we'll deposit the larger sum with you at that time.

Beatrice reaches down to hit the red button to cut the phone call but I grab her wrist and stop her. Bitch, I say in Hindi to Mrs Daniels, you stupid old bitch! Beatrice slams me in the head with her elbow and ends the call and tears the headphones from my ears and shouts, Out! She glares at everyone else, What are you doing standing around, staring like idiots, back to work! She pulls her own headphones off and throws them angrily aside and follows me into the hall. I stand there, in the dim grey light, throbbing from head to toe, filled with rage. I didn't fully know it when I was on the phone, but now I begin to understand. I wanted to hurt her, the widow Daniels, crush her, this mother of five, this woman who was a wife, who is a grandmother, the smugness of her American ease, her American wealth, her sense of place in the world, how much I wanted to sit back and be able to dream of the day she learns of all I would have stolen from her, from all the blind, self-satisfied widows of America.

Beatrice looks at me coldly, her face stiff. Seven thousand, she says, seven thousand dollars and you let it go. She's going to have to tell the Big Man we've made nothing tonight, zero, zilch, nada, he's going throw a volcano-sized fit. He has a wedding coming up, his youngest, she says, he needs the cash, he wants to make it really big. She taps out a cigarette, lights it, and her face relaxes and she says, You really fucked it up, didn't you, then nods towards the end of the hall, indicating we take a walk. Smoke haloes her head as she paces ahead of me and leads me to one of the storerooms. A single bulb hangs from the ceiling. It illuminates the room when she flicks the switch. Shelves are stacked with toilet paper, cleaning supplies, all sorts of useless crap. I think of her in the movie, her body slim, taut, the butterfly almost fluttering, but say nothing. It's a kind of power, knowing it and not saying, and as Susan says, or her guru says, power is truth.

She locks the door from the inside and produces a silver makeup case, opens it and carefully pours out four lines of coke onto one of the metal shelves. Done this? she says, and I say a few times. She rolls a bill and snorts two lines and hands it to me and I snort the other two. She closes her eyes, breathes in deeply. It helps, she says. She doesn't say what that means, what exactly it helps. I feel the thrum of the drug through my nervous system and my pulse quicken. Suddenly everything looks just a little brighter. She jumps onto a wooden crate and smirks and shakes her head. What are we gonna do with you, she says, you pull that shit again. She makes a motion to slice her throat. She relaxes and unzips the fly of her blue jeans and spreads her legs and takes my hand and slides two of my fingers under her panties and inside her. I enjoy how the warm, wet glove of her pussy enfolds me. When I try to move my hand she tightens her grip and stops me and closes her eyes and leans back, clinically guiding my motions. I get the message. I'm just the hand. It doesn't last long, and I don't know if she comes. If she does, she doesn't make a sound. She pulls my hand out and brings it to my face, and wipes my fingers across my nose and cheeks and lips and laughs, a kind of almost hysterical laugh, like we're kids and we've done something really, really wrong, but who cares, right. Her features transform, and for a moment she becomes oddly serious. I think I like you, she says out of nowhere, and adds, That never happens. She jumps down and as she tucks her shirt back into her jeans, I catch a glimpse of the butterfly. There it is, tattooed right below her navel, like a secret promise. C'mon, she says, back to work.

20

FBI Special Agent Jack Christiansen, from the St Louis, Missouri, field office, is the only one of us to make money that night, though even that is a paltry two thousand. It's far past our quitting hour and the regular crew, the actual call centre kids, will arrive soon. As we're filing out, having shut down our computers, the Big Man's roar echoes along the halls, his fist thumping a desk, foot kicking the trash can into the wall. Beatrice appears and stops me. It's obvious she's done more lines. The impact's written across her features, in the cool blankness of her eyes.

He wants to see you, she says, not now, this weekend. She finds a piece of paper and writes out an address and hands it to me. At his house, she says, and adds, His daughter's engagement. I take the paper and pocket it and begin to walk out when she calls from behind. Wear something smart, she tells me, Buy something, he'll pay you back. She pauses and stands there, evaluating me, then runs a finger down my cheek. I'd like to see what happens when you clean up, she says. I turn and wave a finger in the air, acknowledging what she said, and vanish into the corridor.

Special Agent Jack Christiansen is lighting a cigarette when I walk out. A dark muddy grey paints itself against the sky and the air is already heavy. I light my own and nod and am about to move on when he says, Hey bro, and nods back to the building, Wouldn't you like to fuck that, that sweet ass. He means Beatrice, and he's said this to me every time I've shared a cigarette with him. He's a gawky kid with wiry features, his skin dark, and clothes always too big for him. The jacket he wears hangs so ridiculously off his shoulders I want to pull it off, throw it in the trash and slap some sense into him. I give my standard response, Who wouldn't, I say, and he looks at me boldly, pulls himself close and sniffs me in a weird sort of obvious almost dog-like way. He could as easily be sniffing my asshole. I don't move, I just smoke, but I know where this is going and I already don't care. It's a performance and he's about to deliver the punch line.

I can smell her on you, bro, he says, I smell her all over you, that wet pussy all over your lips. His face is an inch from mine and he adds, I heard you, bro, you and the ice bitch laughing, I heard you when I went to piss. He blows smoke into my face. Come on, bro, he says, you gotta share next time, you can't keep all that to yourself, you gotta call me, two guys, bro, one on each end. Instantly, I'm back inside the movie house with the old man, watching that poor wannabe actress get destroyed while all my anger at the Mrs Daniels of the world and their oh-so-cosy lives bubbles back to the surface. I grab his stupid lapels and lift him in that loose piece of shit suit and slam him against the wall. I don't know what I'm doing, what I'm going to do. I think I'm going to punch him in the gut but don't. I know these types too well. It's not her he wants to fuck, it's me, she'd just be the meat sandwiched between the two of us, he just hasn't realised it yet. You want to taste that pussy, I say, and he nods, strangely excited. Here you go, I say, and kiss him hard on the lips, pushing my tongue between his teeth, forcing them apart, deep into his mouth. I can feel him struggling, trying to cry out, his body raging uselessly against mine, but I hold him there, my chest pinning his, our groins pressed against each other, my tongue pushed all the way into him, so deep I can almost lick the back of his skull.

I let him go and push him to the ground. He stares up at me with fear and I watch as he tries to figure out how to get back on his feet. Somehow he can't. It's like he's forgotten how to stand. After a minute, I hold out a hand and he spits on it and knocks it violently away, then suddenly jumps up and looks at me savagely, with a look of ancient disgust in his eyes, or is it terror, I don't know. He's trembling all over, like he doesn't understand what happened, or is happening, and raises an arm and points at me. He just points, not saying a word, slowly walking backwards. Then he turns and begins to run.

He disappears and I tap out another cigarette and light it and turn in the other direction to walk home. In the shifting sands of a Delhi dawn, where grey washes out grey, I taste him, the taste of onions and potato chips and cheap tobacco and saliva, as if he is just one more smell in this lung-choking air, one more ghost haunting the lost minutes before a sun no one will ever see rises.

21

Jaggi is sleeping and Basam is nowhere to be seen. I climb into Jaggi's bunk and let his arm engulf me and cradle my body against his. He grunts and shifts, then starts snoring again, his mouth pressed into my neck, stinking of whisky. He's loud, right in my ears, vibrating my whole body. The sensation soothes me as I fall asleep. I wake to the room's afternoon grey, the chilly air, the sound of Basam's phone squeaking out shrill music. Jaggi is gone, and Basam is sitting, slouched in his bunk, scrolling through his phone. When I climb down to go to the bathroom, he acknowledges me with a dismissive grunt. We made a deal, he calls from the bunk as I'm pissing. I finish and consider him from the toilet doorway. When he speaks he keeps looking down at his phone. You in your bed, the other in his, he says, then things are easy, but this. We made no such deal, but I don't say that. The actual deal was simple, and he's more than a couple of months past keeping up his end of it. I don't like it, he says, this dirty shit. He adds, And where are those shirts? How's a man gonna pound some Gurgaon pussy if he don't have quality shirt?

I take a shower and when I finish, Basam's gone. The air's sharp with his cologne, something cloying and heavy. Then I remember. It's the same scent I smelled on the waiter that night. I'm not surprised they know each other, if that's the case. In Paharganj, we all know each other, I guess, or say we do. I wonder what they were doing together that night. No doubt partying, sharing a local whore. Or each other. I know the Gurgaon story is invented, that Basam's waiting until we get tired of him and find another place, so he can reel in some other sucker to pay the rent.

My phone beeps. It's a message from Beatrice. Don't come into work tonight, she writes, stay away from the building. Nothing else. I slip the phone into my pocket and head out into the city's chaos, in search of, in Beatrice's words, some smart clothes. I usually dress okay, but even then walking into one of Delhi's finer establishments I'm met first with the doorman's misgivings if not his outright hostility. One bars my way with his rifle, something ancient, a single-barrel hunting rifle that looks more ornament than anything that could ever produce real fire. What do you want, he demands, his tone not hiding the fact that he doesn't mean it as a question, just an order to get lost. The rifle butt rests on his enormous belly. His wheezing causes the barrel to shiver as he holds it against me. I ignore the provocation and say, Sir, in my most obsequious Hindustani, I'm looking for a fine suit, and I have heard this shop sells the very finest in the whole city. He eyes me up and down, lowers the rifle, and says, I'm watching you.

How they see it, I don't know. Maybe it's smell. The odour of caste, of class, the aroma of your bank balance. I could be dressed in the finest Armani and there would still be a curl of the lip, eyes narrowed in distrust. An old fella helps me, suspended on his cane, and soon I pick out something fresh, the lines clean, the cloth supple and fine. I pay with the wad of bills Anders left me, and he tells me the alterations will be done by tomorrow afternoon. On the way out, the guard opens the door and bows slightly as I leave and lifts that useless gun to his shoulder in some kind of salute. No doubt the odour of a wad of bills drifted across to him. My phone beeps in my pocket as the door closes behind me. It's Susan. She's sent me an animated emoji of a bright *om* with fireworks going off all around it. Her message reads, You don't pick the mantra, the mantra picks you. I send her back a namaste emoji and she sends me fluttering red hearts that burst out of the corner of my phone.

Basam is in his bunk when I return, head propped on an age-stained pillow, staring as always into his phone. He looks at me when I walk in then looks away and says nothing. How's the job going in Gurgaon? I say, and he ignores the jab but says, How's your new job? with an odd twist of meaning in his tone, You know, the one you go to nights, not the one Jaggi pimps you for. I'm here to have another shower, peel some of Delhi's stink off my skin, and change shirts, so this time I ignore him. I don't know how he knows about the other job, I don't talk about it, not even to Jaggi, not here at least. Basam's eyes are red and it's obvious he's stoned from the way he talks, the slur in his voice, the way he extends certain vowels. Come on, he says, tell me about it, tell me about the phone calls, the phone calls to the widows in America. I stop and stare at him. What are you talking about? I say, and he says, turning full to face me, Is this you, FBI Special Agent Bob Masters?

He throws me his phone and I catch it and sit down and stare at the screen. The story's from an American news site. The headline reads FBI WARNS OF RISING INDIAN CALL CENTER FRAUD. There's an accompanying image showing several men and women standing at a news conference, all in various uniforms. What is this? I say, but he just stares, the hint of a smile forming on his lips. There's a new gang of telephone fraud artists working out of New Delhi, India's capital city, the article states, who've developed a particularly effective system. Not only are their techniques unique, one of the FBI agent says, but they're genuinely convincing to an unusually high percentage of their target population, mostly elderly widows, women who wake up the next morning to discover they've been defrauded out of as much as tens of thousands of dollars, right out of their bank accounts and with their authorisation. The article goes on to detail the technique, and the warning signs to look out for. It's all there, everything I do, everything I set up for Mr Harbans Singh Alhuwalia and his nameless crew. The chummy greetings, the local details, the emphasis on contacting other family members to discuss, the secure government bank account, all of it.

Basam watches my face as I read. I realise what he's waiting for when I reach the end. That's where the kicker arrives. In cooperation with Indian authorities, the FBI have identified one of the ring leaders, perhaps the mastermind, the one they believe goes by the pseudonym FBI Special Agent Bob Masters. They are currently liaising with New Delhi Police, who have positively identified the individual in question as an Indian national and will shortly be bringing him into custody. They've cleared releasing this information with Indian authorities who have assured them the gang leader stands no chance of escape. As we speak, one of the agents says, the individual is not only under constant surveillance but is also surrounded at all times. I stare from the phone to Basam in disbelief, then throw it back to him and grab mine. No new messages from Beatrice. I slip my shoes back on and run out. Behind me Basam shouts, They've got you, brother, got you by the balls! I run down the stairs and into the street and I can still hear him laughing.

It's quiet this time of day. A few hawkers, a man ironing clothes under a tree, someone sleeping next to their ice cream cart. Dogs laze in the drowsy heat and I wonder where all the eyes are, watching me, following me, waiting to pounce. Do they expect me to lead them to the office, to show them where the gang works? But if they've been following me for so long, they must know. I dial Beatrice's number but there's no answer. I try Mr Harbans Singh.

The same. They must know, and have vanished. I'm the sacrifice. Either that or they've been picked up already. I take the path that goes west under the overground metro tracks where families slumber in groups and cycle rickshaws dodge the always angry drivers. A girl of maybe five contorts herself amid the stopped traffic of a long red light, hoping for a handful of paise. When the light changes and the traffic charges on, she snakes her way back to the median, where she slumps and waits for the next red. I try Beatrice again. Again nothing. I don't want to call Jaggi, I don't want him caught with me.

The streets around the office are quiet. A few drowsing guards, dogs hiding under cars, a family camped in a construction site under a makeshift canopy. There's no sign of checkpoints, police, anything unusual. I don't know why I've come here, especially after Beatrice's warning. But if the article Basam showed me is correct, there's no hope anyhow. I might as well be discovered at the scene of the crime. I approach the building's glass doors and notice something in the reflection. A man sitting on a bench with a newspaper, but he's not reading, he's staring at me. I turn and look at him and he looks away. There must be a dozen others, in their cars, watching from rooftops, casually strolling the street. I climb the stairs and reach our floor. The silence is eerie. I have a key for the call centre room and open the door and walk inside. The air conditioner is off and the room is stifling, the air thick. I leave it like that. In the bathroom I splash my face with water and drink from the tap, and stand there, staring at myself in the mirror. I form a gun with a hand and shoot my reflection a couple of times. I wish I had a gun. If they're coming for me, I want to go out in a blaze. I imagine bullets hitting computer screens, shattering windows, my body riddled with them, squirming like an epileptic as I go down. By nighttime, there's still no sign of anyone, no footsteps in the hall, no doors beaten down. I surf the web, hoping for news. Nothing. Jaggi calls. I ignore it. Finally I curl back into my corner and fall asleep. It's easy somehow. With death only hours away, all other questions are answered or irrelevant.

22

In a dream I'm swimming through dark waters, murky waters, waters that suggest a sky, a sun, maybe a moon, but it's at best a blur, an idea or a memory that once there was a sun, a moon, a sky, that once there was a surface to the water. The world is green or black and I move forward, twisting as I swim. There is no up, there is no down, there is just space, water, darkness. Something moves towards me, a shadow in the distance, darkness against darkness, growing larger, and I wonder, as the shape engulfs my vision, how is it I can breathe, breathe in a world without air.

23

I wake to a series of texts from Beatrice. The air is sticky but cool and I wash my face in the bathroom before looking at the phone. There're mostly a bunch of smiley faces. Obviously something worked out. But who for? The alarm is over, she writes, the call centre will shut down, but not to worry, they'll take care of me. She sends links to a news story from local papers along with a bunch of laughing crying emojis, as if what I'm about to read is hilarious. The headline reads INTERNATIONAL FRAUD MASTERMIND PERISHES IN DRAMATIC ESCAPE ATTEMPT.

A joint operation by the Delhi Police and the National Anti-Fraud Task Force arrested the notorious international criminal known as FBI Special Agent Bob Masters in a dramatic nighttime raid. After his booking and while being transferred to a maximum security facility, the international felon attempted escape, at which point the brave officers of the Delhi Police risked their lives to apprehend him a second time. In the ensuing gunfight, the felon known as FBI Special Agent Bob Masters lost his worthless life. No police officers were injured.

There's a statement from the officer in charge, Captain Daksh Deshpande. It reads, This vile scoundrel who defrauded so many American widows will never again do his dirty work on these shores and the widows and their families in America can sleep in peace knowing a phone call from him can never again destroy their savings or their peace of mind. There is a note to say the notorious felon's real identity has not yet been established and members of the public who recognise him are encouraged to come forward. Relevant authorities are actively pursuing the possibility of links to Pakistan, and to their security forces, which are strongly suspected.

Two photos are attached, one of Captain Daksh Deshpande and the other a mugshot of the felon Bob Masters. The portrait of Deshpande is formal, well-lit, his moustache perfectly twined at its ends, his expression fierce, commanding, the whole thing airbrushed into boyish lifelessness. The mugshot of Bob Masters shows a battered face, with obvious bruises, a nose that looks like it's collided with more than a couple of brick walls in the previous hour, and eyes as much in shock as they are lost. I know those eyes. I saw them two night's ago. It's FBI Special Agent Jack Christiansen. I can still taste his mouth, still smell his skin. I start to laugh. I can't help it. I fall on the floor and laugh. Laugh and cry. Like I'm a living emoji. I lie there, staring at the ceiling, laughing and crying, not knowing what either means, what the laughter means, what the tears mean, until I can't laugh or cry anymore.

24

The fat-bellied guard welcomes me this time, thrusting that useless rifle onto his shoulder and attempting a salute before he holds the door open. Jaggi is with me and the store is empty except for the crowd of hennaed or bewigged octogenarian shop assistants. Jaggi checks out the ties while I go to the counter to collect my suit. The same cane-suspended shop assistant approaches and insists I try the suit on, just to make sure. The process takes half an hour, and when I leave, it feels like walking out of a mausoleum, the dead air of the vault still clinging to my shoulders.

Jaggi says he wants to have kulfi and knows a shop in Saket. We call out to a passing auto and climb in. The wind whips our hair into our eyes and Jaggi shows me the half-dozen ties he lifted as I was checking the fit and asks which one is my favorite. I pick a bright yellow one, and he ties it around his neck, badly, so he looks like a thoughtless school kid. He ties another around mine, a shimmering golden one, equally sloppily. Look at us, he says, grabbing the driver's shoulder and forcing him to turn around. Brothers in ties! The driver is unimpressed, and returns to navigating the city's chaos.

The market is crowded and before we look for the ice cream shop, Jaggi buys a bottle of whisky. He slips it into his shirt, so it hangs there, like a second belly. He looks ridiculous, with the bottle and the yellow tie, but no one seems to take much notice, except the odd guard, who eyes us warily as we saunter past. Jaggi makes a face at each of them, then stops at a sari shop. Look at this, running his finger through the delicate fabrics. The owner is a smartly dressed middle-aged woman who appears and asks what we're doing. Jaggi tells her we're looking for chunnis, but not just any chunnis, the very finest she has, like the fabled silks of old Kashmir. She asks who they're for and he throws his arms wide. Who do you think, madam? he cries, tossing his head back and promenading back and forth, looking more ridiculous still. I don't know what's got into him but I'm enjoying the game. To my surprise the owner laughs, really laughs, getting into the spirit.

We try on one chunni after another, sometimes two or three together, tying them around each other's heads, admiring, commenting. Jaggi produces the bottle and we share a few sips. The owner pulls us into the store and in the cool dark takes a long drink. You are very naughty boys, she says in a loud whisper, and giggles, and we are outside again, with Jaggi wearing five or six of her finest scarves on his head. He starts to dance, something modern, and sing too. I don't recognise the song, and then I do. Lady Gaga, the one about the telephone. He does it perfectly. He must have been practicing in secret, because I've never heard him sing it before. A crowd gathers, even a couple of the suspicious guards join and watch. I forget sometimes how good a singer he is, how good a performer. Why he does what he does and not this, I don't know, he's never said. He never speaks about himself, and I realise I know nothing about him, where he was born, if he was educated, if he remembers his parents or not, if he has siblings. The crowd is clapping along and Jaggi grows more animated, holding an invisible microphone to his lips.

When it's over, he takes a bow and the crowd applauds. He raises the invisible microphone high before dramatically letting it drop. This causes another round of applause, and we retreat into the store and share more whisky with the owner. There are tears in her eyes, and she rubs Jaggi's thick thighs between her hands. I've never seen anything like it, she enthuses, why are you not on television? She goes on and on, you should be a star, if you were a son of mine I would be so proud, on television you never see anything so good these days, you are a real talent, India's great talent. Jaggi picks out two of the scarves and offers to buy them, but she refuses any payment, they are a gift, she says, excitedly, her voice high and nervous. He ties one carefully around my head, and I tie the other around his, and then he leans forward and does something he has never done in front of a stranger, maybe not in front of anyone. He kisses me full on the lips, like a lover, in a way he almost never kisses me. When he pulls away, the woman takes us in her arms and hugs us, pulling us tight into her, and I think, as she's holding me, is this how a mother holds a child.

25

We lie on a grass embankment abandoned between highways. Contorted steel sculptures rise from small hillocks on all sides as the traffic roars. We forgot about the ice cream and bought more whisky and wandered out among the boulevards wearing our chunnis, arms linked at our elbows. There's an old song I remember, I saw it on television but don't remember where, two tramps on stage walking arm in arm down an avenue. Maybe Fred Astaire and Judy Garland, but I don't know where the memory comes from, how old I was, why it's stayed so long, hidden inside me, waiting to reappear now. Jaggi passes me the bottle and we watch the grey smog hiding the grey clouds, and Jaggi says, Soon, with all the money we've saved, we'll go south, we'll swim in the ocean, we'll rent a house, just the two of us, climb trees and pick coconuts and crack them open and drink the water until it spills over our faces and across our chests.

He talks on and on, like the woman in the shop, about all the things we'll be able to do now we have money, real money, he means the money from my job, and all the places we'll go, not just south but north, into the mountains, where the air is clear and cool, where there's snow, real snow in winter, where you can climb and climb and you're still staring at the tallest mountains on the planet, at great rock beasts so massive they crowd out the sky, even there, at the very top of the world. I listen, saying little, enjoying his enthusiasm, and fall asleep to the whisky, the sound of his voice, of the traffic punching the air around us. When I wake it's night and the bright lights of cars cut into my eyes. Jaggi is gone, having left the empty bottle standing on the grass as a memorial to this day.

26

The red jacketed servant ushers me along the hall before depositing me in a mansion-like living room. I immediately realise I've seen it before. The room is crowded, heavy with voices. I search for a familiar face and spot Beatrice walking towards me with a broad smile. She looks gorgeous, radiant, in a yellow and green gown, flashy and new, low-cut at the front so it displays a plunging arrow of cleavage and completely bare at the back. She hugs me quickly, then steps back, dropping her palms in admiration. Look at you, handsome, she says, guess there was a man hiding behind the boy. We still don't know each other's names and I can't call her Beatrice so I whisper, asking what her name is. She laughs, of course, and tells me, Kavita. I tell her mine, and she kisses me on the cheek and runs a hand lightly along my ass. Come on, big boy, she says, the Big Man's waiting.

French windows rise along one wall, looking out onto a vast walled garden, lush and well-maintained, with palm trees and ponds and a fountain. Inside, enormous plants spread their leaves across an arrangement of velvet couches while a mammoth chandelier dominates the ceiling. The couches have changed, but otherwise the room remains largely the same. It's the room from the movie with Beatrice, or Kavita, if that is her name. It's hard not to picture the other room, the one in the movie, with the couches set in a semicircle while the women pound themselves senseless on the cocks of strange men. I wonder if any of those men are here. Their faces were mostly hidden, so even if they are, I wouldn't recognise them. Around us, splendidly sareed women sit alongside a few elderly sardars while the Big Man's sister spreads herself out while being fanned indulgently with the corner of a large banana leaf. She sighs so loudly she can be heard above the din. A sort of soft jazz raag fusion plays in the background and photographers and videographers roam, making a record of the scene. Two thrones are set up at one end, an arch of flowers stretching over them, where the future husband and wife will sit during the ceremony.

One of the photographers stops us and we pose, arms around each other's waists, like a young, handsome couple, and push on, through the throng, through hallways and rooms, until we reach a glassed-in solarium, complete with short gravel paths and ornate wrought iron benches amid the lush greenery. I hear the Big Man's voice before I see him. He emerges from behind a banana leaf, and despite the recent turmoil, looks genuinely pleased to see me. He throws his arms wide, Welcome, welcome, he cries, my star employee, then looks around sheepishly as if to check if anyone is listening, and bellows, FBI Special Agent Bob Masters himself! A figure appears behind him, a smartly dressed police officer, and Mr Harbans Singh turns, looks horrified, Oh no, oh no, he cries out, throwing his hands into the air, we've been discovered!

The figure is Captain Daksh Deshpande himself, complete with manicured whiskers and a dress uniform with golden epaulets and chestful of medals. Well, well, well, the captain declares theatrically swinging his stick through the air, who do we have here, not the notorious international criminal mastermind Bob Masters, but I thought we killed him, I thought we shot the dirty little rotter in the back. Taking my chin in his hand, he examines me closely, and says, excitedly, It is, it is, we have him finally, the real one, then grabs me by the shoulders and roars with laughter, slaps me on the back, and congratulates me. I've been following your work for months, he says, I've never heard anything like it, genius, he says, a real Einstein in our ranks, and found in the dung heap. He wraps an arm around my shoulders and says, Walk with me, and to the Big Man's objections he says, Don't worry, you'll have your little boy wonder back soon.

We follow a short path that snakes behind a cluster of banana trees while he talks, not letting me say a word. He's in awe, genuine awe, because not only have I made an extraordinary sum for Mr Harbans Singh, but I have created a whole new fraud, a new category of fraud, it's never been done before, and I did it out of the blue, he still can't quite believe it, the potential my method has, because if they can replicate it successfully across several cities, and even taking into account a loss of fifty percent effectivity without me personally on the phone, the ROI he projects is astronomical. I don't know what ROI means and he says, of course, you're not a businessman, it means return on investment. Initial capital investment and training will naturally be expensive, but once the operations are running they'll be cash cows. Cash cows, he cries out, waving his stick in the air, and you, he adds, FBI Special Agent Bob Masters, will have your finger in every single pie. He leans in and whispers, Or dick in every single pussy, just think about that.

I ask what really happened to the other Bob Masters, the one they shot, and he says I shouldn't worry about that, they never thought for an instant of actually going after me, but the Americans had got my name and once the Americans have a name they must have a body, it's an old rule, and it always works, besides, he was some nobody from the Northeast, no one will remember him, except they will now, as the international criminal Bob Masters, you could say it's the best thing that ever happened to him, and of course he's a gift that keeps on giving, we'll be looking at his sim card soon and we've already decided we're going to find phone contacts with suspected ISI agents in Pakistan, that will really get the press frothing, plus, he says, dropping his voice to a whisper again, abhorrent sexual practices, men, boys, who knows, animals, it's amazing, he concludes, grabbing me and pressing me against his chest, how much value can be squeezed out of a well-planned death!

27

The ceremony is beginning and the Big Man tells me he'll see me in his office later, he means his office here, and nods vaguely at the ceiling. I follow Beatrice to one of the bathrooms, all gold fittings and marble and mirrors staring into mirrors. She taps out lines of coke on the countertop and we snort a couple each. I see my reflection on the glistening marble as I inhale the lines. I'm a god made of stone, I tell myself, and raise my head to be met with an infinity of mes, an endless regression in the facing mirrors, millions, a hundred million, and I think of how this moment repeats itself in every universe across space and time. I laugh and Beatrice asks what I'm laughing at but I can't explain. She hitches herself up onto the counter and pushes my hand into her. She's wet, and I rub her quickly. She comes almost instantly. She throws her head back and thrusts my other hand into her mouth to stop herself from crying out. She takes my face in her hands and kisses me. I want to fuck you so bad, she says, rubbing her nose against mine, but later, huh.

The small gurdwara is built into the house and when we reach it the ceremony has begun. The granthi intones from the Guru Granth while the bride and groom sit cross-legged before him, resplendent, glittering, in the richness of their finery. A series of spots have been set up to light them, as if they're actors on a stage. To one side, the big man's sister struggles to remain upright against a wall. The room is crowded and we crush ourselves into the back, Beatrice on the women's side, me on the men's, my shoulders pressed into both my neighbors. I still feel Beatrice's moist skin on my fingers and play the scene over as I watch the betrothal. The ceremony quickly bores me and I focus instead on the faces around me, who look equally bored but struggle to keep their eyes open and intent. We're all playing our parts. Obviously, everyone wants to get back to the food. There's a rumor the bar will open soon, someone says near me, otherwise he's going home. It's met with a grunt of assent. I hear other grumbling. Who does Harbans Singh think he is, it's not like this house is his, or ever will be. There's talk of real estate, what belongs to whom, and something about the sister, but I don't follow it.

Suddenly the Big Man looms over me, pressing a hand into my shoulder, while his crotch drifts close to my face. The ceremony is still going on, but his part is over. He nods for me to follow. Beatrice glances at us, jealous no doubt at our escape. The sister, meanwhile, has given up trying to remain upright and has completely fallen over. She struggles, even then, to keep her head off the floor. I follow him up the grand staircase, its railing painted gold, and reach a landing overwhelmed by a metres-wide framed photograph of the Golden Temple. After a couple more hallways we reach a door marked PRIVATE. He unlocks it and we enter a suite, dominated by an oak desk and leather couches. He locks the door behind us. Other doors lead to a bedroom and a bathroom and a wall of windows look out onto the city's universal grey. My private domain, he says, and switches on the television using the remote. It's a large, flat-screen set, bolted to the wall. The screen fills with an old black and white Bollywood number, from the fifties or sixties, but the sound is off so I don't know the song. I wonder if it's one of the ones Jaggi sings. He pours us both whiskeys and tells me to sit down. On the wall behind the desk hangs the portrait of his father, the one used at the funeral. He has taken off the plastic, and the corner protectors. The old man stares down at us morosely as the Big Man talks.

Dull business, isn't it, he says, I don't know why we do it, go through all this for what, they'll have a few weeks of pleasure, maybe some months, then what, she'll be pregnant and he'll be visiting whores, the way it always is. He takes a drink and stands and walks to his desk and picks up one of the framed photographs and hands it to me. It's his wife, young, beautiful, an astounding beauty, piercing eyes and a delicate mouth and something steadfast, real, about her. Just looking at her you know she's standing somehow on solid ground, that there's not a flighty thought in her head. A love marriage, he says, and laughs at himself, can you believe that, me in love, and with her. I'd seen her downstairs, from a distance, and she hadn't lost her beauty, or her figure. The few glimpses I caught she seemed to float in that room, from person to person, a ministering angel.

She's no doubt crying now, he says, the last of her babies getting married, and to a good man, trust me, he is, or he is today, what he is tomorrow is none of our business, because every man is a good man on his wedding day, is he not? He talks on like this, refilling our glasses when they get low, and says he disapproved, indicating the photograph of his father, he was very angry, because it meant his choice was ignored, and his choice was the daughter of his childhood buddy, his school chum, the friend of his bosom, he had dreamt for years how the families would be united and so when I fell for Amrit over his choice he was furious, all his hopes dashed, and so was his friend, they never talked again those two. Huh, he grunts, friends. We eloped, he says, I was twenty-five and she twenty-one, perfect age for both of us, I'd sown some oats and she still knew nothing of the world, a blank slate for me to write my name across or anything else I chose. We had a good sex life for a while, quite good, I saw few others, I didn't need to, a man gets his urges but in those first years they were rare, blessedly rare, and I thought maybe I am a man changed, a man reformed, a man freed of his demons.

A bass thud begins rumbling through the walls, and he says, The DJ has started, a DJ, scoffing at that, for a day like this, they'll be wondering where I am, let them wonder. I think of Beatrice, her lithe figure dancing to the beat. The Big Man is beginning to exhaust me. I could use another line of coke and wonder if she's serious about fucking later. Maybe she's found someone else in the meantime, one of the men from the movie perhaps. As the Big Man talks, I think of her waist, the butterfly fluttering as she's pounded from below. When the first of the girls arrived he began to soften, he says, he was happy to be a grandfather at last, amazing the power young girls have is it not, but he never forgave me, he blamed the loss of his friend on me, the loss of happiness in his final years, he kept saying imagine me sitting here with Pavan, the two of us sharing whiskies late into the night, that is an old man's life and you robbed me of it, and for what, my old man said, a beautiful face, how long did your happiness last, I could have told you that, and he was right I suppose, in that way old men are always right, but I wouldn't have done it differently, I would still have married Amrit, if only to watch his misery grow.

Well, the old man had a surprise at the end, he says, a real stinger he kept secret, he loved his secrets the bastard. He pours himself a fresh whisky, filling the glass to the brim, and tops up mine. The surprise is this. The house and grounds and all inside go to his sister provided she finds a husband. Failing that, it will remain divided between the two. She's found a husband, he says, that wasn't difficult with all she has to offer, though what he'll do with the fat cow I don't know, pump a baby inside her and lock her up I guess. Or make sure she has an accident a year into the marriage, the usual way. I'm going to lose the house, and everything in it. He downs the last of his whisky and stares at me. I have a small job for you. Maybe you and your friend. I need you to kill her, he says bluntly, and you have to do it soon, the engagement ceremony is next month. If we wait until after there'll be no end to questions and suspicion.

28

As I listened, my anger rose. I'd felt it since arriving, a faraway drumbeat, an approaching storm. The money, the opulence, the blank, bored expressions, the lifelessness of this blood-drained house. Only seeing Beatrice kept me here, and when the Big Man locked the door behind us, it felt like a kind of fate, he is locking a prison door, mine, so when he started to talk I felt sure I knew where he was going. He is going to make me his son and heir, to give me all this, have me call him father, I can hear it at the edge of every word he speaks, a phantom waiting to show itself, this man with three daughters and unable to call a man his son. The idea revolts me, to be called that, to be called brother, to call someone father, mother, sister, to speak of family, aunts, uncles, cousins, the whole sick gang of ancestors and descendants, of property, inheritance, bonds of any sort, it enrages me, and I think, if he makes the offer, if he extends a hand and claims me as family, I will strike him in the face, knock him to the ground and kick him in the head, the old fool who thinks he can make me his son, who thinks he can conjure a family for me out of thin air. I'm trembling inside the more he talks, no one has ever talked to me like this, for so long, so intimately, I grow more and more certain, maybe it's the drugs, the alcohol, but my conviction strengthens, yes, I tell myself, I'll kill the old fool where he stands.

Then he asks me to kill his sister, You and your friend, that Caliban character, he says, and the ground seems to give way under me. I'm certain he says something else, he must have, but he goes on, explaining the money he will give us, an extraordinary sum, and the plan, as simple as can be, and as I listen I start to laugh, it's as if a storm has broken and I'm in the street getting giddily soaked, my body dripping and wet, and I laugh, Of course I'll kill her, I shout, taking him by the shoulders, shaking him, holding him, and we are both laughing now, throwing our heads back with tears in our eyes, Yes yes yes, he shouts, and we jump to our feet and start dancing, clapping our hands, Kill the bitch, he sings, kill the fat fucking whale! We dance like this, spilling the whisky, turning this way and that, like maniac children, when he pauses briefly and gets his phone out and makes a call. It lasts no more than a couple of seconds. All he says is ten minutes. He drops the phone and suddenly grabs me by the shoulders and throws me hard against the desk. I crash into it, my belly taking the full force of the desk's edge, violently winding me. He punches me in the back of the head and slams my face into the wood. You dirty, fucking whore, he shouts, dirty, dirty fucking whore! I know what's coming. A part of me welcomes it.

He pulls my pants down and unties his belt and unbuttons his trousers. He leans forward and presses my head into the desk with his elbow, crushing the side of my face into the wood. I hear him wheezing and smell the sour alcohol unrolling thick on his breath. A whore like you will like this, he says. He pulls back and spits onto my asshole then pushes inside me. He's right, I do like it. Not the pain, which is real, but the anger, the anger of a man who could have taken me just by asking, whose rage demands he rape me. I own something of him, I think, as he punches hard inside me. The low rumble of the DJ rises from below and I see, in the brightly polished sheen of the desk, a reflection of his father's portrait, hanging above us, staring down impassively.

The Big Man grunts, pulls out, spits on my asshole again, and again pushes in, holding me there now with his hands tightly gripping my hips as his breathing grows more laboured. The pain intensifies. None of this is enjoyable except the fact of it, that's he's doing this, and to me, while downstairs his youngest daughter is celebrating her betrothal. A painting of the world as it is, as it's always been. It's good to be reminded. He whispers as he thrusts. At first I don't hear it, not until he grows louder. Then I make out the words. I am a dirty, rotten bastard, he says, I am a dirty, rotten bastard, over and over with each stab of his dick inside me.

I can see the portrait of his father clearly now, along with the shelf below, which holds an incense holder and a brass cup identical to the one he spat the mouthwash into after our encounter at his Karol Bagh office. I remember what it is. A memorial cup, purchased when you cast the ashes of a loved one into the river. So that's what he spat into, his father's memory. His thrusts increase, and his voice rises and he takes hold of my neck and slams my forehead into the desk. I am a dirty, rotten bastard, he says, louder, and as I feel him coming, he adds, And my father knew it. He shouts it out, I am a dirty, rotten bastard and my father knew it, I am a dirty, rotten bastard and my father knew it! He explodes inside me and the middle-aged heap of his body collapses onto mine.

He pulls out and stands and someone unlocks the door. It's Beatrice. He timed it perfectly. She moves quickly, ignoring me, it's as if I'm not here, going first to the bathroom where she finds a bottle of antiseptic, which she opens and pours generously onto a towel, then in front of him gets onto her knees and uses it to clean him thoroughly. He doesn't move, still breathing hard, and stares into the wall. I can hear him, under his breath, repeating the mantra, I am a dirty, rotten bastard and my father knew it. These rich guys, I think, each one a fucking drama queen. From the bedroom, Beatrice produces a fresh suit, identical to the one he is wearing, and helps him change his clothes. The whole time he repeats the phrase. The television is still on. A couple dance among the columns of an ancient temple, Greek or something, and I think of the gods and their blessings, and their curses too, and who are we to question them. I pull my underpants and trousers up and pour myself another whisky and take it to the window. My whole body is sore, pulsing from the assault, and I move with difficulty. The party has migrated outside and his wife and daughter are laughing together in Delhi's charade of afternoon light. When I look back at him there are tears in his eyes. So he did cry, just like I knew he would.

29

Beatrice leads me through the dance floor. It's mostly deserted. Only a couple of young people, moving listlessly, are dancing, while others sit on chairs, talking amongst themselves. We enter the garden. His sister has been carried out and lounges on some sort of divan. A servant shades her with a parasol and another fans her with an ostrich feather. She looks like an ancient queen, dropping chocolates into her mouth, which she plucks from a silver tray. Serious-looking sardars are everywhere with their whiskies and their turbans. I recognise many faces from the funeral. Beatrice has done a couple more lines since I last saw her. She looks wild, almost malicious, as she pulls me forward. We enter a small group, and there is the Big Man's wife, smiling broadly with her newly betrothed daughter, both of them radiant. Everyone looks listless or blank except these two, who are laughing together.

The Big Man's wife looks at Beatrice quizzically, and Beatrice says she just wanted to introduce me, the Big Man's new star employee. He's been doing amazing things, Beatrice says, profits are through the roof. Amrit turns to me and smiles and holds out a hand, offering the softest handshake I've ever felt with barely our fingers touching. I'm always glad to meet members of the staff, she says, especially such obviously valuable ones. Beatrice can't help herself. He really is a miracle, she says, Harbans is one hundred percent behind him, you could say he's thrusting him all the way to the top. She starts to giggle and can't stop, and drops her head onto my shoulder, mumbling apologies but still laughing. It was a joke, I explain, I was telling as we were walking over. Amrit nods, but I know she doesn't believe me. Her voice cracks when she says that no doubt it's not the kind of joke that can be shared in mixed company. As we turn away, what radiance there was in her face is gone, and she glances around anxiously, looking for her husband I assume, who is nowhere to be found.

Captain Daksh Deshpande grabs me by the shoulders and pulls me away, saying I'm his now, she can have him back when we're finished talking men's business. He leads me to the drinks table and gets us both large whiskies without asking if I want one, and we toast the happy couple. Call me Captain, he says, it's what everyone calls me, even my children. We walk, his arm wrapped jovially around me, I have a good feeling about you, he says, a very good feeling, when I look at you I think of my sons. He pulls me tighter and I already want to get away. He lowers his voice. I'm sure the boss man has told you our little problem, he says, there's nothing for you to worry about, I'll take care of any complications with the law, you can be sure of that, we have to protect such a prized asset as yourself.

We make a slow circle among the trees that leads us back to where the sister lies, gorging on sweets. She looks up at the Captain sourly and says, Why is no one talking to me today, I sit here and no one talks to me. The blank-faced servant fans her absently and she strikes him with the back of a hand. Don't be such a lazy ass, she cries, do you know how hot it is out here. He speeds up momentarily, then drops back again. There are no good servants anymore, she announces, none at all, and look at us, how are we expected to live, it's like they want us to live like dogs with none of the comforts of our ancestors, what do you think Captain, we should have a few whipped as an example, maybe at India Gate, the undeserving wretches, so everyone can watch. She nods to the servant fanning her. Maybe this one, she says, but I doubt his back is strong enough to take the whip. She unwraps and pops a chocolate into her mouth and the servant stares on impassively.

Neither the Captain nor I have said a word, and the Captain now bows slightly and says, Madam, I wanted to introduce to you this young man, one of your brother's colleagues, a truly talented young man. She squints and tells me to come closer and grabs my tie and pulls me to her until I am inches from her face. It's obvious she's started using whitening creams, or procedures, no doubt for her upcoming engagement, but all it's done is made a mockery of her features, a white mask sloppily painted across a collapsed face.

Colleague, she laughs, my brother has no colleagues, only sycophants and servants, and which one are you, what kind of bootlicker, eh? Her eyes move across my face as if she is examining every pore. It's funny, she says, I can smell him on you, so you must be a bootlicker. She pushes me away and turns back to the captain. Why do you bring him here? she asks, and before he can answer, she says, I'll tell you why, because there's no hiding anything from me, the old fool's in trouble isn't he, what's he done this time and how did this young man save him, there's no other reason he'd be here, among us, the family, taxes is it, or worse, something to do with your people, you useless police, what happened, eh, a burglary, was the business ransacked, did this young man stand up to the thugs, did he fight them off while my stupid brother shitted himself in the toilet, that's the story, isn't it, that's what makes him so valuable?

She spits into the grass and looks at me again, My brother's Prince Valiant, she concludes scornfully, riding in on your white horse, saving that idiot, but I don't know why you bother, he'll hang himself one day, hang himself with his own schemes, isn't that right, Captain, you know more about that than anyone else, because you're an intimate, aren't you, you're deep in his counsel, which I never was, the old fool never talks to me, never so much as says good morning, what kind of brother is that, I'll tell you what kind, no brother at all, just a ghost, and what kind of life is the life of a ghost? She coughs and demands water. One of the red-jacketed servants runs over, carrying a glass and she drinks it quickly. You waited long enough, she says, did you hope I was going to choke, did you think you'd get out of your duty? The servant stands silently until she flicks him away with a wrist. None of them talk to me, she says, do you see that, it's like the servants are all mute, what kind of upbringing must they have had, I mean if they can't even say a few kind words.

The Captain bows again, it's been a great pleasure, he says, pulling me away, I'm sure we'll have time to talk at length later. You're not going, she cries, we're having such a good time, real conversation for a change, not like these chattering ninnies in the garden, oh please, she beseeches, stay with me, just to timepass, everyone needs a timepass, then turns angry, Well go, do as you like, leave me with these wretches for servants, you'll see, my brother will hang himself with his schemes and where will you be, don't look to me to help! We hear her from meters away and I turn to see her lying again on her back, staring at the sky, raging at the air. The Captain tightens his grip. You understand now, he says, the kind of creature she is, why we cannot allow this house, this great family's legacy, to fall into her hands and whatever scoundrel she dug up for a husband. Beatrice strides towards me across the grass and I have never been happier to see her. Before she pulls me away, the Captain claps me on both shoulders. You're family now, he insists emphatically, never forget that, FAMILY!

30

The future bride and groom are dancing, arms draped over each other, and move in slow, wide circles across the floor, staring into each other's eyes. We're sitting on chairs pushed up against the wall, watching them. They're a handsome couple, and for a moment I let my cynicism drop and wonder if maybe, just maybe, they might be happy. He's not a bad man, Beatrice says to my speculations, educated in the US, American citizen, and he's got a good job, in Italy, they'll move there after the wedding, to Turin, a real city, that's a life, isn't it, she'll be away from all this at least. I don't know what a life is except my own, and that's not much of one, maybe none at all. I don't say this, but stand and walk to a wall of family photographs.

The father, the mother, the children, grandparents, uncles, aunts, cousins, a clan of connections and roots, the web that binds people's lives. Except for me, I think, all I have is a single strand, not even that, just a dot, me, myself, I. Several of the photographs show Harbans and his sister, whose name I still don't know, how young they look, almost happy, but what surprises me is they look identical, except the clothes they're wearing and the cut of their hair. I take a closer look and realise what seemed so eerie in looking at her earlier, the sister, what I couldn't put my finger on until now. They're twins, born together, and look at them now.

You noticed, Beatrice says, coming up behind me, I can see it on your face. Romulus and Remus, I say, and she looks at me blankly, so I add, Aurangzeb and Dara Shikoh. But they weren't twins, she says, and then says, laughing, India and Pakistan. She stands behind me and slides a hand into my trousers until I feel her finger searching for my asshole. You made me a promise, she whispers, come on. I'm so tired and drunk and buzzed I can barely stand and my ass is still sore, but I allow her to lead me away. As we're leaving Mr Harbans Singh appears and takes his daughter's hand. We pause and watch for a moment as the pair dance, a father and daughter, in the fading evening light.

Beatrice finds one of the hidden bathrooms, lost among the hallways, where no one will disturb us. We do a couple of more lines and she sits me on the toilet seat. My tired little boy, she says, what a big day he's had, don't worry, I'll perk you up. She sucks me until I'm hard, it takes minutes, then loosens the string on her pants and mounts me, moving slowly up and down. I let her do it, it's like I'm not there, I'm nothing except a stiffened rod for her pleasure. We hear a noise at the door and a moment later I see behind her a small white dog. It lets out a low growl followed by a series of barks. Maxim, Beatrice cries, stop that, and she turns to me, He never barks, not like that, it must be all the commotion. The dog won't stop, and finally Beatrice pulls herself off me and chases Maxim out and locks the door this time. He whines for a minute at the door then goes quiet.

Do you test? she says riding me. Test, I say, what do you mean? She rolls her eyes at the obvious. I shake my head, No, I don't. She grabs my shoulders, Bad boy, bad boy, I hate condoms so I'll have to suck you off at the end. I ask if the Big Man tests, and she laughs, Him, test! No, he doesn't test, she says, he has a better method, he fucks his wife once a month and has her tested, it's the only way he can do it, he tells her they're routine blood tests, borderline diabetes that's got to be monitored, blah blah

blah, his wife gets those results but the HIV result comes to me, she knows nothing about it.

I start falling asleep and she bites me on the neck, No you don't, and moves more vigorously, pumping me. I pull up her top up so I can see the butterfly and she pulls it off completely and now pounds me and I watch her compact breasts and mouth but most of all I watch the butterfly. It flutters and soon flies, detaching itself, and circles her head, rising to the ceiling, around the lights and back again, and following it, I feel a kind of dislocation mixed with wonder, at her, this world, the strangeness of this thing called life.

31

The only thing Jaggi says when I tell him the Big Man's plan is, When do we do it? It's early morning and I'm lying in his arms and it's just the two of us in the room. His breath warms my neck and I can feel his cock, half-erect, pressing against my ass. I'm surprised how cool he is about it, but I'm still often surprised by Jaggi. It's been two years since we met, not in a movie theater like I told Susan, but at a small club in South Delhi, where I watched him sing and fell in love there and then, like in the movies, as much with his voice as his body or face.

He moved from patron to patron, stopping briefly at each one, letting his voice roll over them. When he arrived at me, our eyes locked and I couldn't help but turn to jelly. He stood there during the remainder of the song, singing to me and only me. The room disappeared, so did the stinking city, everything, the world itself vanished. There was only Jaggi. Jaggi and me. When he finished, he reached forward and kissed the top of my head. That kiss sent an electric jolt through my body. I wonder at how he can show such tenderness yet be indifferent to the idea of murdering a stranger.

The night of the new moon, I say, when it's dark in the garden. He runs his fingers lightly across my face and kisses my ear. Don't worry, little bird, he says, with that kind of money we'll be free. I press my back into his chest and allow his arms to swallow me, and like that I fall asleep. When I wake he's gone, as he often is, and Basam is lying in his bunk, watching porn, the phone held high. I ignore it and go wash my face and when I return, he's turned the sound up loud. The tinny squeak of flesh slamming flesh fills the room, along with the tortured cries of a woman. This is a good one, he says, Bihari porn is the best, those fucking bastards they make their wives do anything.

I'm walking out the door and he calls out, Eh brother, good shoes no, Adidas, or Nike better. He raises his feet to show me his battered running shoes, the soles peeling off. Who can walk around like this on a new job, he says. I nod and say I'll try and he says, Don't try, do, man, what point of trying if you don't do, stop this bullshit talking and take action, steal the fuckers. I say nothing and leave and think maybe I'll just buy him the fucking shoes. The air's sticky and I start coughing the moment I'm on the street. I drink tea and buy a Red Bull and drink it in one gulp and hail an auto-rickshaw to take me back to the Big Man's house. I want to look at the garden walls, see how fool proof this plan of his looks. Before I get out I untie my shoelaces and walk like this, the laces flapping, along the street.

The street sweepers are out, bent over as they move dirt from one side of the road to the other while the ones on the far side move it back again, making the air thick with dust. The few guards around stare blankly at passing vehicles and I follow the high wall surrounding the Big Man's compound. Ivy or some kind of plant hangs down along its side while the top is crusted with shards of shattered glass. The door is where the Big Man said it would be, a sturdy metal door secured by an interior bolt, invisible from the street.

I bend down to tie my laces and take a closer look. The plan is absurdly simple: he will leave the door unbolted. That's it, the whole sum of it. The hinges look half rusted and I wonder how easy it will be to pull the door free. I know I can't tell him to have one of the servants oil it. That would bring attention. Opposite is a mansion, something new and flashy, rising out of the street like one of those cruise liners, with its own freshly-built guard station. The ivy, or whatever it is, covering the door will hide us in the dark if we have to play with the door. Laces tied, I walk quickly on and turn the far corner. The traffic has come to a horn-blaring halt. The end of the road is blocked by a police cruiser with its lights flashing. I walk along the sidewalk, treacherous with tree roots and smashed paving stones, as the traffic thickens and grows louder. A minute passes before some VVIP in a black SUV shoots past. The cop car blares its siren and follows and the stalled traffic spills again into the now empty street like a drunk vomiting into a gutter.

32

Basam is gone and I pull the box from its bag and toss it onto his bunk. I gave up and decided to buy them at the mall in Vasant Kunj. Along with a half-dozen shirts. All of them fancy. I'm about to be rich, what do I care. I change my mind and pull the Nikes from the box and arrange them on his blanket, side by side, like a pair of happy siblings, but seeing them there like that something flips inside me and I think fuck Basam, fuck his asshole demands. I find the shawl I stole for him and throw it between the shoes and pull the shirts out of their plastic wrapping and throw them across his bed. I unzip my pants and pull my dick out and piss onto everything, the shoes, the shawl, the shirts, then all over the bed, making sure to leave some for his pillow. I laugh to myself knowing he'll think Jaggi did it, and he'll come after Jaggi and Jaggi will drop him like the sack of shit he is. I can already see the blood spilling down Basam's ugly mug from his soon-to-be smashed-in nose.

33

Beatrice offers the shallowest of waves from across the parking lot and I navigate the bleating horns of two-wheelers and fatass cars to reach her. Instead of kissing or hugging, we nod to each other, a pair of conspirators, and begin a slow walk along the market's mostly ruptured sidewalks. She's carrying an oversized handbag swung from her shoulder and wearing a new perfume and the moment the scent hits me I'm lost in the tangle of her flesh, the taste of her sweat, and I see the butterfly again, fluttering higher, as both of us leave our bodies. The demands of a beggar bring me down to earth and I'm surprised to see Beatrice give the old woman a bill. The money instantly vanishes into a tortured fist while eyes telegraph dissatisfaction with the sum. The beggar moves on, muttering about the injustice. Beatrice shrugs when I question her, answering, We all need to make a living.

A week from Friday, Beatrice tells me matter-of-factly, eleven at night, she'll be outside in the garden alone and there'll be no moon, no light at all. The Big Man already explained. The sister walks at night, always night, always alone, not even a servant with her, using a walker. She hates being seen like that, with the walker, and that's the only exercise she gets, if you can call it exercise. Don't worry, Beatrice says, you won't even need to see her she breathes so loud, like the fucking elephant she is. It all seems almost perfect. I nod my agreement and Beatrice points to one of the flashy dessert stores and suggests we get coffee and cake. Inside it is bright and gold and yellow and pink, with sickly light pouring in waves from the ceiling. We take our seats at a small round table, also gold and yellow, and the waiter appears with menus. There are so many choices I can hardly make sense of it and I'm about to tell Beatrice to order for me when the waiter comes back. He can see the confusion in my eyes, the fact that I'm little more than a shipwrecked drifter in their tiny world of overwhelming abundance. I instantly hate him.

What would the sir like? the waiter says, in his most obsequious voice, and I look down at the menu, at the long lists of desserts and coffees, none of which I know anything about, and bring my finger very slowly to the first. This, I say, the sir would like this. He nods and turns to Beatrice, who says she'll have the same. He begins to walk away but I call him back. And this, I say, equally slowly, placing my finger on the next menu item. Beatrice adds, Me too. The waiter nods and leaves and again I call him back. This time I bring my finger down ever so slowly until I am pointing to the third menu item. Beatrice giggles and adds, Me too. This goes on for a couple of more rounds, both of us now giggling like stoned teenagers, while the waiter's exasperation rises. His jaw clenches and body stiffens each time he turns as I call out to him. Finally, the manager strides over. He's a large man, with a dyed black moustache, which twitches as he talks, and dull eyes and the faintest strands of hair heroically combed over his bald head. Is there a problem, sir, he says, you seem to be ordering many dishes, perhaps you would like to take some home? I tell him there's no problem, that I don't want to take any home, that I want to eat them, all of them here, at this table, and I want them now.

His anger too is rising, and I like watching it, the slow boil painting itself across his face in the quickening twitch of his moustache, the tightening squeeze of his lips. There is no reason to have a tone with me, sir, he says, this is a fine bakery, the finest in Delhi, and we are proud of our products, we just want to make sure you have the maximum enjoyment, if you understand, and I worry that with so much food you will not soon be able to appreciate how excellent it truly is. I say nothing for a long while, simply staring at him wordlessly, until he says, Sir? and again, Sir? and finally I say, Do you know who I am, and he says, No sir, I do not have that particular pleasure, and I say, I am Special Agent Bob Masters, of the

Federal Bureau of Investigations, and Special Agent Bob Masters wants his desserts, he wants all of his desserts, and he wants them now! His body starts to shake, his mouth clamps tightly shut, and he stands there, the moustache twitching wildly, until finally he says, As you wish, sir, your order will arrive as quickly as we can possibly prepare it.

He turns in a rush, almost tripping, and the sight of him, his humiliation, sends us back into our peals of childish laughter, which we force ourselves to suppress. There are limits even to our juvenile cruelty. Orders are shouted, and the plates arrive, one after the other, the most opulent desserts I've ever seen, piled high with cream and nuts and honey and syrups, all of them garish and ugly, like the place itself, a lunacy of puke-worthy colour. The waiter brings a second table, to house the overflow, and this too quickly fills up. Everyone in the room is watching, the children pointing, giggling among themselves, while a few take photos with their phones. I stare at Beatrice across this opulence. None of it looks appetising, and I confess to her, I don't like sweets, I never have. She takes a spoon and dips it into the cream and feeds me. How is that? she asks, and I say, I don't know, I can't taste it. She tries the next, feeding me again, and again all I taste is a cloying, almost suffocating sweetness, otherwise flavorless, a sort of sugary cardboard I tell her.

Soon she has fed me a spoonful of every dessert, and I can hardly tell the difference. None of it excites me. Nothing, Beatrice says, and I nod, Nothing, I say, and for the first time she looks at me with a kind of curiosity bordering on pity, as if asking herself, who am I, who is this person sitting next to her, what made me and what drew us together. She hasn't tried a single mouthful, and she rises, calmly taking my hand, and leads me to the counter. She asks for the bill. The clerk looks astonished, as does the manager, who approaches, looking worried. We will wrap it all, he says, but Beatrice is adamant. Just the bill, she says, and adds, Everything was excellent, too good to eat more than a mouthful, that's why we ordered so many, we knew it would be like this. The manager's face softens, almost melts with happiness. Thank you, he says, handing her the total, You are welcome anytime. She pays. As we walk out, she takes my hand and tightens her grip as we walk through the door, like we're a real couple, not a pair of crooks, and when I look at her in the harsh Delhi light, there's a tear in her eye. A real tear in a real eye. She brushes it away, and says, Let's get a fucking drink.

34

We drink tall beers in a dark, first floor bar with a brightly lit fish tank sitting forlorn in the middle of the room, but with no fish in it, and a lot of men, all men actually, other than Beatrice, hunched mostly over whiskies, each glass drowning in soda or warm water. A cricket match silently plays on the flat screen television, but no one is watching except the staff, who stand, necks craned, trying their best to ignore the regulars. The beers are cold, glistening from perspiration. Somehow all the laughter we shared at the bakery has been punched out of us, and we sit now, morose and agitated, unsure what just happened. Neither of us say anything until finally Beatrice says, I used to be in movies, you know, I mean not that kind of movie, the other kind, I mean the kind where I get fucked, I mean fucked a lot, like all the time. She says it strange, like it matters to her what I think. I'm surprised she cares. Then it's my turn not to say anything, and I see the nervousness form in crisp lines around her eyes, and finally I say that I know, I've seen her. I tell her the story, or some of it, and recognising the Big Man's house when I visited for the party, and seeing the butterfly, first on the screen and then on her.

That was the day she met the Big Man, she says, he was there, but watching, and a few of the men in the movie were also at the party the other day. The shoot was organised as a gang bang for his friends, went on for hours, every one of the women fucked in every hole how many times she couldn't guess, but of course, always hiding the men's faces. We talk about the movie, the men there, her first months working for the Big Man, learning how to find the right kind of boy, skinny and young, but not too young, he doesn't like children, she says, she means no one under fourteen, and dirty, he likes them

126

dirty right off the street, she says, and better still if they're not pros, he hates it when the pros pretend, act up like a faggot once they're alone with him. She stands and does a quick sashay back and forth, head thrown up, and we both laugh, and yeah, she says, answering my question, he always cries at the end, and if I'm around, she says, and I almost always am, I'm the one who cleans him up, he won't let the boys touch him once he comes, then they're just trash off the street. My job is to pay them and get rid of them as quickly as possible.

As she talks, she peels the label first from her beer, then from mine, and then from the two we follow up with. I've never noticed her fingers before, their delicacy, the sky blue nail polish glinting in the light cast by the fish tank. She's wearing bangles, cheap and plastic, but on her they look cool, perfect, and a simple gold band, like the one I took from the old guy in the cinema, and I realise suddenly how well dressed she is, the new perfume, her hair just so, the confession about the movies, and begin to think this is a set up of some sort, that she's building to a question or proposal. We switch to a quarter of whisky, served in a glass jug with ice on the side, no soda, and go through it so quickly we order another, along with kebabs and french fries. The food fails to counter the alcohol and soon my head begins to swim. That doesn't stop me from ordering more whisky. She asks about my past, the nuns, what's she heard from the Big Man, and I laugh, The nuns, he told you about the nuns?

Maybe it's the whisky, maybe it's her scent drifting across the table, the memory of sex, who knows, but something in me shifts and I break my one rule and tell her about myself. The story's the same as a thousand others. Solid, uptight family, proper Indian middle class, richer than most. A couple of sisters, aunts, uncles, nanny, driver, cook, and a fancy car for Dad. Maybe even some version of love. Until my mother walks in on me with my mouth wrapped around my cousin's dick. I was fourteen, he was sixteen, we were figuring shit out. Anyhow, all boys military academy for me. What a joke. Within a week I'd had dicks stuffed into every hole. A month passes and I'm the headmaster's personal bitch. He really liked my ass. Ran away at the end of the year. I left with two skills. I could read and write English. And I could fuck like an A-class whore. Guess which one made me more money. Beatrice clinks her glass against mine. Did you ever see them again? she asks. She means my family. I shake my head, No. My sister got married, the younger one. It was in the papers, the gossip pages. She married some halfway famous Bollywood star. In the bios I read, it always lists her as having only one sibling, an older sister, no brothers. So yeah, I say, the orphan part's true.

That reminds me, she says, have you seen it yet? I look at her blankly. Seen what? She rummages inside her handbag and pulls out one of the city's glossy weeklies and lays it on the table. This, she says, it came out today. I look at the cover in disbelief. There is Jaggi, striding across a photographic studio stage, holding a microphone, and grinning that unbeatable Jaggi smile at the camera. He's dressed in a brilliant red and gold sari, one that looks expensive, very expensive, and is made up more beautifully than I've ever seen him. You can feel the energy pulsing off him from the photo. The headline reads: India's Next Superstar? I flip the pages and find the article. There's a half dozen photos of Jaggi, all studio shots, all immaculate, and in each he's sporting a different outfit. The writer's name is Madeleine St. Marie. No doubt the woman Madame Yoyo pointed out to me, the Frenchie journo. She wasn't writing about the club. Her prey was always Jaggi. I scan it quickly. His voice, his looks, his extraordinary stage presence. Something about being an orphan, poverty, rising from nothing, always making it on his own. Singing only in underground clubs, hole in the wall places. Then the kicker. A major recording deal in the works, but still under wraps.

A record deal? Beatrice says, and I say, Yeah, and lying, add, We can't talk about it but Jaggi's really excited. Be careful, she says, that world swallows you whole and spits you out like you're nothing. I nod, still staring in disbelief at the article, trying to hide my surprise. When did all this happen? When did the photo shoot take place? Or shoots? How did the writer even hear about him? And the recording deal. Is it real, is it something Jaggi or the writer invented? It must be real, I think, otherwise the article makes no sense. No doubt they hired her to build buzz before the announcement. I talk generally, pretending to know the details, but the whole time I'm laughing inside, that Jaggi could keep this hidden, and for so long. Was he planning to surprise me? Or just Jaggi being his secretive self? I push the thoughts aside and when Beatrice asks, tell her not to worry, that he'll be there, by my side, when we meet the Big Man's sister.

Her family was like mine, she says, bringing us back to where we started, middle class, upper middle, whatever. Elite private school, the kind where as soon as you turn sixteen the cocaine's flowing and you say hello to the boys by sucking them off. But instead of pulling it together after graduation, or pretending to, you know, she says, fake college, fake job, fake boobs, fake marriage, fake kids, weekly drinks at the gymkhana and fucking the Pilates instructor just to remind yourself you have a pulse, for reasons beyond her comprehension she just kept on sliding. She laughs, relishing the ironies. Weirdly, she says, it was working for the Big Man that put some order back in her life, got her off smack if nothing else, like he offered her a new world, an island world of crooks and their schemes, a protected little paradise. I'll call you Miranda, I say, not Beatrice, and quote the line, How beautiful mankind is, o brave new world, that has such people in it. She's heard that someplace, doesn't remember where. I tell her about Jaggi's dream, a beach in Kerala, a small house, no worries, just the two of us, the thieving behind us, swimming every day, plucking fruit from the trees.

She takes my hand and strokes the palm. She doesn't believe in dreams, or fabled beaches. The Big Man showed her the only things that matter. Money. And power. That's all you need. That's all that exists. That is the whole world. She's drunk, and she knows it, she says, but ... You and me, she says, why not. Why not what? I say. She laughs and begins to dig a nail into my palm. You know what, she says. She adds, We make a great team. Forget some beach house, in a year we'd have enough for villas in Mumbai and Himachal. The sea and the mountains. We'd fly from one to the other in our own helicopters. She releases my hand and I drink more whisky and the world softens and I fall into a reverie, the three of us, if Jaggi's still around, just like she says, master criminals in our faraway villas. Is this the set-up I feared, her dream of us, has she already built the villas in her mind, does she go home each night and see us, just me and her, in our Mumbai aerie, drinking martinis a mile above the wretched and the poor? So goes the evening, we drink, we dream, we fade into the woodwork, a pair of orphans on a raft, floating from where to where, who knows, but clutching onto each other as the night ages and the sky darkens.

A couple of hours later I leave Beatrice in a cab and sway through the headlight-drunk streets, alcohol strumming its happy tune through my veins, having told myself one of my long walks through Delhi's night air is exactly what I need to clear my head. There's so much to think about. Not just the sister, but Jaggi. I have so many questions I can't begin to think of all of them. I lurch from side to side, avoiding pot holes and tree roots, letting the cool breeze revive me, and then I feel it, the sharp blow and the crashing pain. Something slams hard into the back of my skull and the world goes truly dark.

35

I open my eyes and see blurs, colours sliding into colours, shapes into shapes. Everything spins and my head throbs. Forms emerge slowly, ones I gradually recognise. A door, two walls tight on both sides, a grimy, stinking floor. I'm in a toilet, hands handcuffed behind me to the toilet's base. The edge of the seat digs into my back and I hear water in the pipes, and faraway, throbbing through the floor and walls, the sound of thudding rock music. My ribs are in agony. Someone kicked me a dozen times or more. Each breath feels like a knife stabbing into me. The door is shut, but there's a gap under the stall. I reach my head down to take a look. Pain shoots through my body with each movement. There's nothing except what I'd expect. The base of urinals, other stalls, the main door far away. Everything stinks of urine, including me. My hair is wet and so are my clothes. They've taken a piss on me, or several. A burning ache spreads across my face and I pass out or fall asleep, I'm not sure which. When I wake I hear voices. The voices are outside, beyond the outer door.

I strain my body to look under the stall but this time the pain is too much. Everything is foggy, out of focus, my head feels ten times its usual size. They must have drugged me. I don't know how long I've been asleep. I smell a fresh round of piss on me. The music is gone, and the silence feels like a blanket's been thrown over the world. I struggle with the handcuffs but the pain only worsens and I let out a loud cry. A minute later, I hear the door open and footsteps approach. A shadow stretches across the floor and I see shoes outside the stall door. Cheap men's shoes, not even leather, covered in dust, already falling apart. The figure stands, unmoving, and spits onto the floor. After that, he walks away and this time the light goes off. I hadn't even realised the light was on. I slump down in the darkness. Light leaks from under the far door, and slowly my eyes adjust. Here I am, I think, tied to a fucking toilet.

I bang the handcuffs loud against the porcelain and try to shout. All that comes out is a hoarse cry. They must have punched me in the throat, and hard. I slam my feet against the tiles, then slam them at the door. It flies open, and there is the bathroom, with me trapped inside. The light from under the far door goes out and the room goes black and I hear footsteps walk away. I try the cuffs, doing everything I can to pull my wrists free, but nothing. They're as tight as can be. I'd have to break a wrist.

The darkness magnifies the pain, and I slip in and out of consciousness, sometimes dreaming, sometimes not. I'm swimming again, through dark waters, and ahead lies a sunken ship, one of those old ships, out of an old story, with masts and made of wood, tilted half on its side, at the bottom of the ocean. Figures are struggling, trapped, still drowning so deep underwater, how are they still alive, how are they still drowning, how am I, but no matter how hard I swim, I can't reach them, deep currents throw me back, more powerful each time, until I'm desperate, panicking and thrashing wildly.

36

I wake to a flashlight so bright it slices into my eyes. I can't make out the figure holding it. A wiry fella is all I see. It must be the guy with the cheap shoes. He says nothing, just stands there, holding the flashlight in my face. When my eyes begin to adjust he brings it closer, blinding me again. I hear him take a step forward and unzip his pants. I thrash my legs but can't do anything from the angle I'm tied in. A stream of piss lands on my chest, then he angles it onto my face. He giggles softly to himself as it runs across my hair and eyes and down my chin. I've heard that voice before but can't think where. My memories are all fog. The light goes out and his footsteps retreat and the far door opens and shuts. Once again, I'm left alone, in the dark, with no idea what time it is, or day, or how or when these goons are planning to kill me. Or why.

37

The flashlight again, as bright as before, with the same wiry figure holding it. He doesn't say a word, just blinds me. I start to thrash around, expecting him to piss on me. This time he doesn't move, doesn't even move the flashlight forward as my eyes adjust, simply stands, staring like a fucking cow. Soon I make out the shoes, those cheap fake leather pieces of crap. I've seen them somewhere too, I know I have, but my mind is haze, I can barely form a thought. Who are you, motherfucker, I say, scratching through the words. At least my voice is back. There's that laugh again, thin and stupid, and I know him, I'm sure now, but each time I'm close to placing him my mind goes blank and it's as if I don't have a past, or I've lost it like a lost coat. I don't have anything, just this cracking voice demanding to know who it is, who is in this void of a fucking toilet with me. I stretch out my legs, trying to kick him, but can't reach. Motherfucker, I shout, who the fuck are you! The light goes out and he spits onto the floor and whispers, Faggot, and starts to walk away. Then I know it, I know it instantly, who this fucker is. I start shouting, slamming my wrists forward, kicking the ground and air. Motherfucker, you motherfucker, I'll kill you you motherfucker, over and over. By then he's gone, the far door shut and I'm alone lying in this motherfucker's piss screaming into the dark.

38

I take my left wrist in my right hand as best I can and slam it hard into the floor. Pain explodes through my arm. I do this again and again. Finally I hear a bone crack. I faint from the pain. When I come to, my heart is pounding and sweat is pouring down my face. I start again and pull and pull. Each time it sends my hand into a new agony. An hour passes, maybe more, and still I'm trapped as pain explodes throughout my body. I sit there, staring into blackness, panting like a dog in summer. I'm so thirsty I can hardly breathe. I let my body fall as far as it can. My wrist is nothing but agony. I crane my neck forward and bring my face as close as possible to the floor, letting the full weight of my torso force my body down. I've smelled nothing but urine since being here, but the smell is suddenly overwhelming. I reach out my tongue, trying to taste anything liquid. Every inch of me screams. Even then I can't reach. I can't even drink the motherfucker's piss. A day, who knows, two days, ago, I was dreaming of my Mumbai villa, and here I am, desperate to drink piss off a toilet floor. I pull myself up and, for the first time since I don't know when, I cry. Real tears. Where's that water coming from, I ask myself. I capture a few drops on my tongue. It tastes like an ocean. My head collapses forward and the world vanishes.

39

I wake to pain shooting up my left arm. I can't guess the state of the hand, or how badly I've broken the bones. There's a voice outside, and light from the hallway leaks from under the door. The line of sinks almost glows with a supernatural radiance. Whoever is in the hallway is talking on the phone. Strangely, my head feels clear. Maybe he forgot to drug me again. Or I've reached a state of near death clarity. Either way, I know the voice, I'm sure of it, even garbled through the door. The light goes out and the door opens and a flashlight flicks on. The narrow beam searches the floor and finds my stall. It climbs my body until it lands full on my face. I know you, I say, I know who you are. There's another long silence while he walks forward, bringing the flashlight closer. Soon I hear that thin, reedy voice again. It doesn't matter, he says, you think a faggot like you is going to live through the day? He adds, Or your faggot boyfriend?

At the mention of Jaggi, I thrash against the restraints, and start shouting, demanding to know what he's talking about. Somehow I manage to reach a leg out and kick him, ignoring the spasms of pain. He jumps back and starts laughing that idiot laugh of his, and I hear him unzip his pants once more. Then it happens. Suddenly, I am free. I don't know how, but my broken hand slips through the handcuffs and I fly forward. There's no pain anymore, just me, a human fist. I throw myself at him as he lets out a scream. The flashlight goes flying across the floor, sending its beam in wild arcs, spinning before it comes to a halt. I throw him down and with my left elbow crush his throat while punching him with my right. I can't feel a thing, no pain at all, all I am is a body twisted into fury. What have you done, I scream into his face, motherfucker, what have you done!

His legs kick under me and between my punches he lets out weak, pleading cries, begging me to stop. Please, sir, he cries, each time he has a moment, don't kill me, sir. I see his features now, outlined in reflected light bouncing off the wall. The waiter from the fucking Paharganj café. All this just for the bullshit I put him through, it makes no sense. I hold my fist back and put pressure on his throat. Why are you doing this, I say, tell me motherfucker. He

138

says nothing and I punch him hard. Please, sir, he cries, they make me, he make me, your fucking friend. I punch him again. What fucking friend, I say. Please, sir, no more punches, he begs. I want to punch him but stop. I'll show you, okay, he wheezes, just let me go, let my neck go, I can't breathe, I can't breathe. He goes on like this, blood dripping from his stupid nose, and he looks so dumb and ugly I can't even look at him myself. I raise my elbow and he coughs and sputters and sits up, and I lean my back against one of the stall doors. The pain floods back into my body and the room begins to swim.

I climb to my feet and the waiter tries to rise so I kick him and tell him to stay the fuck down. There's blood smeared across the floor and I almost slip. I make it to one of the sinks and take a long drink from the faucet, gripping the edge with my right hand to keep myself steady while my left arm hangs limp. Each motion is agony, even breathing, but the flood of water through my system feels like a monsoon. It takes a long time for me to reach forward and switch the tap off, and when I do I push myself upright again and turn. The waiter is standing, right behind me. I get ready to aim a fist but he raises his arms and takes a step back. Do you want to know, he says between coughs, where your friend is? I grip the side of the sink to keep myself upright and nod. Okay, he says, just stand there. There's blood covering his chin and his white shirt is soaked in it and I can see it's not easy for him to stand either. He reaches into his pocket and produces a phone. I recognise it as mine. I sent him a message, he says, he will call sir, any minute now.

He hands me the phone and I take it, not sure what's going on. He will call, the waiter repeats, and I look at him confused. Who will call? I say, and think, he means Jaggi, Jaggi will call, he's messaged him and he's coming, he's coming here. I'm overcome with exhaustion and I slump against the sink, holding the phone like a talisman. Jaggi, I say, Jaggi will call? My legs grow weak and I slide to the floor, still staring into the phone, and sit there uncomfortably, the sink pressing into my neck. The waiter says nothing, and when I look up he's gone. I hear his thin laugh. He's standing at the door and there's nothing I can do. What strength I had is gone. I can barely move my legs. I try to climb to my feet but I slide forward and sprawl across the tiles. The waiter walks away, still laughing, and I watch him close the door behind him. I push myself up with one arm but collapse again, crying out, Stop. I'm not even sure why I want him to stop or why I'm holding my phone. Then it rings.

40

I don't recognise the number. As the phone rings I keep staring at it until it goes silent. I don't understand what's happening. After a minute it rings again. This time instinctively I answer. It's a video call. Jaggi, I say, looking stupidly into the screen. I can't see or hear anyone. The phone moves through a blank room with scarred concrete walls and old boxes and trash piled in corners until it lands on a battered, wooden chair. Sitting on the chair is a pair of running shoes. Brand new Nikes, looking like a married couple seated on a bus. It takes me a few seconds to recognise them, to remember where I saw them before. The past has been sucked out of me and there is no present left that makes sense. Over the back of the chair hangs a shawl. When I finally recognise the objects I continue to stare, still uncomprehending, and think, why is someone showing them to me, what do they have to do with any of this? Jaggi, I say, is that you?

The phone remains still, framing the shoes and the shawl. I think I hear a voice and the phone starts to move. It pans across the room. A table, a small stove and gas cylinder, and on the wall taped cut-out photos of Bollywood actresses. At last it lands on a figure. His face is covered by a hood. I know instantly it's Jaggi. The chair's heavy, metal of some sort, and his chest bound in a knot of wires. The sight of him clears my head. Jaggi, I say, then more urgently, Jaggi. He moves his head, raising it towards my voice. There's blood on his T-shirt and jeans. Another figure comes into view, but I can't see the head. I don't need to. It's obvious who it is. Basam. He stands behind Jaggi and slowly raises the hood clear. Jaggi's mouth is gagged, but I can see his eyes recognising me. Or one of his eyes. The other is so swollen it's closed up. His nose looks broken and his upper lip and cheeks are badly cut.

I know it's you, Basam, I say, croaking out the words. I don't want to think about how Basam captured Jaggi, or how he moved him to wherever he is. Water is dripping from a pipe somewhere, and I hear other voices, men talking quietly to each other. So it took a group of them. I sit up and say, Show your face, Basam. He lowers himself into the frame until his head is adjacent Jaggi's. He's grinning. What you think, he says, how many did we need? I don't answer him. Not five, not even four, he says, three of us, and this faggot was on his knees sucking all our cocks. The camera shakes and there's laughter from the room. We fucked him, every one of us, he says, the fucker was a good little bitch. All we had to do, he says, is send him the photo of you tied up in a fucking toilet, and ask him if he ever wants to see your worthless face alive again. The little fucker came running and in seconds he was on his knees, Basam laughs, sucking us all off. Oh baby, oh baby, he mocks, don't hurt my baby! True love, he says, didn't believe a faggot could love like that, but this faggot, the way he sucked, just so he could see your ugly face one more time.

Basam takes Jaggi's face in his hands and says, Ain't that true, you sucked us all off because of the real thing, love, you motherfucker. Jaggi's one eye stares at me, like the two of us are talking in silence, and the gulf, the distance, it all vanishes, and for a second I'm in his arms, he's holding me, I'm holding him. And then I know it, I know it from his stillness. They're going to kill him. What else can they do? The madhouse logic of the situation demands it. And they're going to do it right now. Because I pissed on a pair of shoes. There's nothing I or Jaggi can do to stop them.

I tell Basam he's had fun, now he needs to let Jaggi go, or leave and tell me where he is and I'll find him and free him. That's the problem, Basam says, because if he lets him go what do I think will happen next, do I think Jaggi will walk away, go back to his life and pretend none of this happened? No, Basam says, Jaggi will come after me, he will come and keep coming, the bastard will never stop, he won't stop until I'm dead, so what should I do, how do I fix this problem, this problem called Jaggi? No matter how much I promise Jaggi won't, that he has my word, that we've learned our lesson, that we're leaving Delhi anyhow, going south, finding a beach, disappearing into the ocean, Basam shakes his head. Is any of this true? he asks Jaggi, and takes Jaggi's head in his hands and shakes it from side to side. Look, he says, even Jaggi says you're lying. We go back and forth, talking like this, knowing the talk is useless, nothing but empty words, that this scene ends only one way. In all my life, I have never wanted anything more than this scene not to end the way we all know it will end, the only possible way it can.

Let him talk, I tell Basam, let him say it. Basam waits, and says, Why not? Let's hear what India's next superstar has to say. He lets out a mocking laugh, stupidly mocking, like he's an actor in a bad movie, and he unties the gag and releases Jaggi's mouth. There he is, my Jaggi, my crazy love, if that's what this feeling is, looking directly at me with one good eye. All I can think about are his arms, being wrapped in them, one last time. Jaggi, I say softly. He stares through a geography of bruises and says, The bastard's right, I won't stop, not ever, not until he's dead. Then he smiles, it's that great Jaggi smile, the smile of someone no one can kill. Remember this, little bird, he says, they jumped me, he's not lying, it only took three, and I sucked all their dicks because I thought maybe that way they won't kill me yet and I'll see you again, just once, and there you are. He throws me a kiss with his lips and starts to hum, it's one of the old songs, a favorite of mine. Soon he is singing, and I'm gone, I'm not in that washroom, I'm not in the building, I'm floating higher and higher, above the city, beyond the smog, and I see it, the planet's curve like a man's sensuous hip lying on a bed, and beyond it the stars. The knife appears out of nowhere. It's in Basam's hand and then it's slicing across Jaggi's throat. Blood pours out and Jaggi's head drops to the side. That's it. I keep holding the phone, just staring. Then someone on the other end clicks it off and the screen goes dark and I'm alone and the world is silent.

144

41

The shoes, Anders says, and I say, Yes, the shoes, and he says, Over a pair of fucking shoes that you fucking bought him, and I say, Yes, shoes I bought him, and he says, That shit is fucked up, and I laugh, I actually laugh, because Anders never says anything like that, something a normal person might say. Laughing hurts so much I'm forced to stop and take a breath, which hurts as much, and I lie there, in the bathtub, a human bruise, as he washes dried blood and urine from my body. He works diligently, soaping me with a large, natural sponge. I'm surprised at how meticulous he is, attentive to the smallest reaction or sign of pain. He checks my ribs one by one. He thinks none are broken, just badly bruised. When he's finished, he takes my penis in his hand and holds it like it's a precious object. I've missed it, he says, and quickly adds, I mean you. He lifts me bodily out of the bathtub and dripping wet carries me along the hall and into the bedroom, where he lays me across the bed, soaking the sheets. No one has ever treated me like this. I want to squirm out of his arms as he walks, but the pain will be too much.

He dries me and dresses the wounds. As he works, he tells me his father was a doctor, something called a GP in a small town in Maine. He'd sit in the surgery as a kid, watching everything, even the women taking their clothes off. They teased him sometimes, flashing a nipple, thinking it very funny, like they were corrupting a minor. He liked it better when the men took their clothes off but never said that. He only stopped when he started getting hardons he couldn't hide, with all the wrong people in the room of course. He expertly splints and bandages my right hand and asks me again to tell him the story. We've gone over it half a dozen times already, but he wants to keep hearing it, or have me keep telling it.

I don't know why I called him first and not Beatrice. Maybe I didn't want Beatrice to see me like this, or maybe I don't trust her yet, or trust her at all, even for something like this, just to find me. I was lucky, he told me, he'd only just got back to Delhi a day ago. I don't remember the phone call, or how I told him to find me. I guessed I climbed out onto the street somehow and figured out where I was, but he says no, I was still in the washroom. He has friends, he says, the right kind of friends. They located my phone somewhere in the building, and he searched the whole place. It was abandoned, the doors were open, dogs were roaming in the dark. A party happened there recently. Trash was all over the place. He found me by dialing my phone and listening for the ringtone. I was lying on the floor, staring into the ringing screen, humming a song. He doesn't know what, but now guesses it was the song Jaggi sang at the end.

42

I mostly sleep. Sometimes I wake and hear Anders in the other room, talking on the phone, or find him sitting up in bed, watching cartoons with the sound muted. Often he sits next to me, working on his laptop or reading a book. When he's on the computer I watch his face through the haze of semi-sleep, glowing in the screen's light. He's given me tranquilizers for the pain. Sometime I try to ask what he's reading but the words don't come out and I fade back into dreams. Or one dream. The same dream. Over and over. I'm swimming through murky waters, with shafts of light slicing down from far above. There is no shipwreck, there are no drowning sailors, and I am alone, and lost, as the beams of light begin to diminish until on all sides there is nothing but darkness.

43

Anders says I've been talking in my sleep. Mostly sounds and sometimes words, nothing he can make out. He recorded most of it on one of his phones. He plays it back for me. I lie in the heady glow of the tranquilizers, in the softest bed I've ever slept in, trying to make sense of my own voice talking back to me from his phone. It's just grunts and shouts, and the outline of a word or a sentence, but like Anders I don't understand what I'm saying. He says one time I woke screaming. He was in the other room and when he ran in I was sitting bolt upright, eyes wide, screaming. It took him minutes to calm me down, and then I fell asleep like a babe, as peacefully as ever. He'd never seen anything like it.

He finds the scream and plays it back. I've never heard myself like this. It sounds like someone else, someone foreign, from a horror movie. He says I'm still in shock, and I don't know, I don't know what shock looks like. I tell him I've probably been in shock most of my life, because except for the pain this doesn't feel different. He'll run tests when I'm back on my feet, but this, he means what he recorded while I slept, has been giving him surprising results. I have no idea what he's talking about. I'm too tired to question him, and drift back into dreams of swimming through darkness.

44

I wake and it's nighttime. It's always nightime here with the curtains always drawn. I check the clock to make sure.

Night in Delhi

Three in the morning. The pain is mostly gone and my head feels clearer. Light leaks from under the bedroom door. Anders must be up. I pull on a dressing gown and go to the toilet for a piss and then out into the hall. My legs feel weak, but otherwise the pain in my chest has almost vanished. He was right. No broken ribs. I find Anders sitting in a small office. I've never seen this room before. In front of him are arranged three computer screens, each showing something different. He's wearing headphones and listening intently. On one of the screens a series of green wave patterns are overlaid on each other, and on another some sort of circle with different coloured wavy bands moving outwards from the centre, and on the last lines of text scroll continuously, so fast no one could possibly read them. The desk is a mess of scattered papers and books, and balancing awkwardly among them are several stained coffee mugs and plates of half-eaten snacks. Empty, crushed bags of chips are piled high behind the screens. He makes notes as he listens and I stand watching for a few minutes before I make a noise by pulling up a chair. He's startled and then smiles. He's glad to see me on my feet, and tells me to pull the chair closer. There's something he wants to show me.

Look at this, he says, pointing to the large circle and indicating what I think is one of the radiating lines. It shows different shades of red, all shifting. The line undulates wildly as it moves from the centre to the periphery, before disappearing off the screen, then reappearing in the centre. His finger follows it the whole way and back to the edge. Do you see? he says, and I look at him bewildered, and he laughs, Of course, how could you? He strikes a few keys and the screen changes. Instead of a circle there's a series of multicoloured lines moving rapidly from right to left, vibrating as they move. A red line appears, seems to swallow the others, then disappears. This goes on and on. What's happening? I say.

You're the red line, he says, and grins at my confusion, Your dreams, I mean, the ones I recorded. I touch the screen and follow the line as it moves. This, I say, and he nods. He used the machine while I was sleeping, recording me the way he had other times. I'm mesmerised by the red, by the shifting shades, how it enlarges, swallowing the other colours, then diminishes and fades away. I begin to laugh, a silly child's laugh, but I have to stop because the pain in my ribs stabs me again. I feel lightheaded and realise I don't remember the last time I ate. I fall onto my side and vomit. All that comes out is a thin, blackish liquid, but the pain of the convulsions shocks my body. I'm sorry, I whisper, and Anders takes hold of me and guides me back to bed. It was too soon, he keeps saying, too soon to show you.

45

I'm sitting upright as Anders spoons soup into my mouth. He looks excited, almost giddy, as if he wants to tell me something but can't, or is holding back for reasons he won't say. After the soup is finished, he insists I sleep, but before I do he wheels in the cart carrying his strange-looking machine. The front shows a series of dials and switches and knobs. He takes his time fitting the headset and attaching electrodes onto my forehead. If I dream I don't remember it, and when I wake, in the dark as always, the electrodes are gone and so is the machine. My phone is sitting on the bedside table. It looks alien, and there's something not right about it. I take hold of it and discover it's not solid, its liquid, pure liquid, dripping down my wrist, red liquid, like blood or the colour of the lines on the screen that Anders said was me. I keep staring at the liquid, not understanding what's happening, and then I see it. I'm holding Jaggi's severed head. I drop it and let out a scream. This time I do wake up. When I open my eyes it's dark, like it always is, and I'm lying there, not making a sound, little more than an indentation in the bed.

46

I'm searching through a pile of newspapers in the living room, half hoping, half dreading that I might find Jaggi's face staring back at me. Then I see it. It's not an image of Jaggi. It's the waiter. The headline reads, MISCREANT DIES IN DRUG GANG KILLING. The report is brief. The body of Pradeep Kapoor, age 24, trainee waiter at Bermuda Café, Paharganj, was discovered in an alley in the Shalimar Bagh district of Delhi. The body displayed multiple stab wounds. The motive is believed to be related to local illicit gang activity. His family or hometown are unknown. The authorities ask anyone with information on the killing, or the victim, to contact them.

Basam is cleaning up loose ends, or the waiter tried to blackmail him, or both. I have so many questions, about Basam, the waiter, how they arranged it so quickly, how they lured Jaggi into a trap. I know I was the bait, a promise of seeing me alive that must've persuaded Jaggi to go along. The questions circle and drift away. I think of Jaggi lying somewhere, alone and unloved, with no one to hold him at the end. I think of his gorgeous flesh rotting, the voice forever stilled. I show Pradeep's photo to Anders. He thinks he's seen him around. I tell him about the night he stopped me not far from here. I wonder, was it here, close by somewhere, in some unknown basement, that they held and killed Jaggi? Maybe his body is lying on a stone floor a short distance away. The thought's oddly comforting. Better than a disused mine god knows where.

Anders hands the newspaper back, still folded over so it shows the article about the waiter. I keep staring at the face. In the grainy newsprint he looks older, almost dignified, a face out of another time. I wonder where they found the photo. I realise I didn't know his name until now. As I lie there, Anders peels back my bathrobe and gingerly pulls my cock out from inside my underwear. It stiffens when he takes it into his mouth. I can't see what he's doing because I'm holding the newspaper up, staring into the waiter's eyes. Then I get it, I know what happened. It's in his eyes somehow. Stupid and obvious. Basam had the waiter tailing me for weeks. How else did he know about the call centre? Assuming I was Bob Masters was a lucky guess. Meeting the waiter at the cafe with Susan was pure chance. Basam was looking for a wedge, something to get me and Jaggi out so he could hook fresh suckers. That's all. I piss on his sneakers and fuck it all up. And Jaggi dies. When I come I'm still staring into the waiter's face, the face of Pradeep Kapoor, age 24, whose home and family will forever be unknown, and thinking of Jaggi, whose beautiful body, I keep telling myself, lies decaying in an unknown basement barely a few hundred meters from here. All because of me.

47

The red line has changed since the last time Anders showed it to me. You see this, he says, pointing to what he says are shifting tones of scarlet and burgundy. They're so subtle it takes me a minute to distinguish them. When I do, a whole other world opens up. The closer I look the more I see. Swirls within swirls, eddies within eddies, teeming worlds of colour flowing before my eyes, bleeding into each other, shifting, colliding, brightening, darkening. He uses the mouse to highlight a tiny section, no larger than a fingernail. He magnifies it until it fills the screen. The effect is astonishing. What looked like a uniform block of colour becomes alive with shapes, forms, even what look like faces or figures, appearing and disappearing, being born before my eyes and as quickly dying.

What is it? I say, and he says, You. There's a smile on his face. He's beaming, like a proud parent. But to be honest, he adds, he's really not sure himself what it is. He *thinks* it's me. One thing he is certain of is this. It's alive, he says, just like you and me, I mean it's conscious. It can't talk, not yet at least. It communicates through a kind of waking dream. Even if it could talk, he's not sure what kind of language it would use. He tries to explain but nothing of what Anders says makes sense. I look back at the screen, where countless shades of red flow and undulate, are born and vanish, and wonder what he means by life, by living, by consciousness. There's a lot more to tell, he says, but not now, maybe later. He can see by the look in my eyes that I'm exhausted, and it's true, I am, I'm almost falling forward from a sudden need for sleep. I have one question which can't wait. What did he mean when he said it was me, did he mean what he said about it using my dreams, or did he mean something else. He walks me to the bedroom. Just what he meant, he says, that it's me, I'm the red, I was the catalyst, he's sure of it now, I brought it to life.

48

I can no longer tell morning from afternoon from the middle of the night. I don't know how many days I've been here. When Anders returns my phone, I open the bedside drawer and shove it inside. I recoil at how much it reminds me of the dream of Jaggi's head. Before I can look away, the screen lights up for an instant. It's crowded with messages. I shut the drawer as quickly as I can and tell Anders thanks, but I'm not ready, the world can wait.

Later, sitting together drinking coffee, he tells me he's been travelling all over the country, mapping people's dreams. Not just him. He has teams going everywhere. The data they gather, these dream maps, are fed into an artificial intelligence engine he's developed with a group of engineers. It melds the different neural nets into something cohesive, a single dream image that he hopes spans the entire nation. He wants to create a map of what he calls India's collective unconscious. Imagine a map, he says, not just of the views and deeply held beliefs of a nation, but of its very dreams. If you know that, he says, you know everything. The power that comes with it is almost unimaginable. It's what the British did when they arrived, he says, what made it easy for them to conquer the country. They mapped it, all the way from the Himalayas to the far south. For the first time, I hear something unhinged in his voice, on the edge of lost, and I realise how little I really know about him. We walk into the office where the computers are still running. The red now streams across all three screens, filling them completely, moving from one to the next to the last, like a river that's overrun its banks. This isn't the full dream map, he says, that's housed in a data centre outside Delhi. This is a sort of bite-sized clone.

They call the big one, the one in the data centre, The Atlas. They plan to test it in a couple of regional centres, maybe Ahmedabad or Cochin, before the next elections. He doesn't say what he means by test, or why the elections. It has to do with what he calls the psychic geography of a population. The artificial intelligence engine studies, learns, creates its own intersecting and overlying maps of a city's dream geography. The Indian government is funding his research, along with a couple of multinational tech companies. He can't name them but I can probably guess. Once you know the atoms of a society's dreams, you can start pulling them apart, rearranging them, make them into something new.

I don't doubt what he's saying about his research and its funding, or the computers and programs and people and screens bleeding red. But I'm beginning to question if any of it is real, if it is what he says it is—this map, The Atlas, these psychic geographies. It sounds like a dream or mirage, a castle built out of air.

He drops his voice to a whisper as if he doesn't even want the computer to hear. I'm only beginning to understand, he says then corrects himself, *we're* only beginning to understand, the team's quite large, but this is an AI engine, no, he says, let's call it what it is, an AI *life-form*, that we believe has the ability to reach outside of itself, to push inside people's minds, into the deepest levels of their consciousness, yes, into their dreams.

He points to the triad of screens. It's disconnected from the network. This way he can carry out experiments without influencing The Atlas itself. What's running now includes the new data he's gathered from me. I ask if it's magnified, and he says no, the red has taken over completely, meaning me, or some version of me. In this version, he says, you are The Atlas. The change happened after he uploaded the recordings he made after Jaggi's murder. They took over, those dreams, those feelings, but more than took over, they provided a spark, maybe my anger, or my grief, who knows what, but the system had never seen anything like it, the intensity of it. I don't say it, just think it: what about love, my love for Jaggi, what if the red is not rage but passion, why can't that be it, the life-giving force? It was a tipping point, he says, something coalesced and emerged, the new consciousness they've been trying to create. His eyes widen and he loses the appearance of an absent-minded professor. Watching his face as his excitement transforms into something narrower, I wonder again at his sanity. This machine, he says, it's not a machine anymore, or not just a machine. It knows we're here, knows who we are, he's sure of it, it's as alive as me or him.

49

The phone is beeping in the drawer. More messages. I forgot to turn the sound off, or even the phone. I decide to do the latter, expecting rivers of messages from Beatrice or the Big Man. Any messages from them are hidden by a recent string of urgent digital cries in the dark from Susan. I scan quickly through them. All calls for help, each one in all caps. I switch the phone off and throw it back into the drawer. I'm growing to like not knowing what time it is, or day, or whether it's night or day. I don't know if Friday has passed or if maybe someone else has killed the sister. I don't want to check my phone to find out either.

I drift into sleep. I do this several times a day, sleeping for no more than an hour or two. The dream is all darkness, like I'm at the bottom of the ocean, but I can't tell if I'm swimming or not, if there's a shipwreck or not.

I wake to find Anders straddling me. His pants are off and he's masturbating over my face. His balls hang an inch from my lips. Without thinking, I take them in my mouth, and then his cock. He comes almost instantly. His body jerks violently forward and the cum hits the back of my throat. He must have been saving it up. I lick the shaft clean, and he finds his pants and pulls them back on and walks out, not once saying a word. For the first time with him I feel used, as if all he sees me as is a private toy. I'm back at the military academy, the headmaster grabbing my skull and thrusting it at his crotch, whispering, That's the way I like it, boy. I remember the smell. Pungent, like freshly turned earth. My body trembles as I rinse my mouth at the bathroom sink and stand, looking at myself. Fading bruises cover most of my chest and the cuts on my face show thin lines of scabbed skin. The splint is gone but the skin still looks whiter where it was wrapped. I think of Jaggi standing behind me, his arms wrapping around me. The image vanishes and I feel alone. I want to get out of here, the endless night of this apartment, Anders' bizarre experiments, his sexual hungers. Everything conspires to suffocate me.

I know it's a bad idea but I open the drawer, take the phone out and turn it on. A minute passes before the screen lights up. I check the date. Still only Thursday.

There are messages from Beatrice. And the Big Man. But also Captain Deshpande. I don't read them. I know what they say. I don't read Susan's either. Instead I call her. I'm expecting to find her in tears from some crisis with her guru or who knows what, but she's not, she's calm. She's in Delhi, staying at a guest house lost somewhere in the alleys behind the Saket Metro Station. I know the neighborhood. It's poor and squalid. She wants to see me but can't leave the room. She'll explain, but only in person, and for some reason I agree. I need to get out, to see another face. I tell her I'll be there in an hour, thinking it an even dumber idea than turning the phone on in the first place. I dress and tell Anders, and he nods and keeps staring at the three screens with their bright red river of blood pulsing and flowing endlessly from right to left.

50

I spend quarter of an hour dodging scooters and navigating crowded alleys before I find the Blue Plum Guest House and Restaurant. I see no sign of any restaurant, just a battered door rising next to a pile of garbage. The door is mostly barred by a sodden mound of sand where dogs lie sleeping. I ignore the dogs and climb over the sand, then climb a narrow staircase that grows steeper the higher I go.

The stairs continue past the first floor, turning a couple of tight corners, and keep climbing. Finally I reach a landing where an empty plastic chair sits behind a broken down wooden desk. The calendar on the wall is two years old. There is a television playing somewhere behind a closed door and the hall is busy with flies. An old ledger sits open on the desk, alongside a metal cup crawling with ants.

On the phone, Susan told me her room number. I find it on the next floor. As I raise my hand to knock, a figure looms out of the far darkness of the hall. A middle-aged man in nothing but his underwear. He pushes past me as if I'm not there, coughing loudly as he walks. I knock and say my name, and seconds later I hear Susan's footsteps scurry across wooden floorboards and the inside bolt slide free. The door flies open and her hand rushes out to grab my arm. She pulls me inside and slams the door behind her, pushing it closed with her back, and stands there, staring at me for a long minute until finally she relaxes, bolts the door shut, and steps towards me and wraps me in her arms. At first I don't know what's happening, then I understand as she pulls me towards the narrow bed. All the while she doesn't say a word, not even a greeting. When I try to talk, she presses a finger against my lips. She strips her clothes off and instructs me with her eyes to do the same. She climbs onto the bed and lies down lengthwise and arranges her arms rigidly at her sides. Her head lies on the pillow, staring straight up, her neck stiff and unmoving. She looks laid out like a sacrifice at some dumb ancient rite. She uses her eyes to indicate that she wants me to fuck her. Right here, right now. I open my mouth to protest, to ask what this is all about, but she breaks her pose and raises a finger to her lips and shakes her head. It's clear from her face that this is not a negotiation.

The bed is little wider than a cot and with no headboard, just the wall, and seeing her lying there, despite her breasts, she looks like a child, no more than thirteen, with her hair cut short and a face that seems to be saying nothing, nothing at all. There's not a hint of desire in her eyes, and I have no idea why we're doing this. Or why I go along. I feel like a puppet, but who's pulling the strings? The ghosts of old purple bruises are apparent across her chest and shoulders, mirroring my own, though some on her look fresh. I'm not hard, and nothing about her excites me, so I think first of Jaggi and then push him from my mind. All I can think about is his body lying abandoned on a stone floor. I switch to Beatrice. That helps and I straddle Susan's belly and stroke myself as she watches impassively. I think of the butterfly and Beatrice's naked chest as she mounted me at the Big Man's house. Soon I've got a hardon and I lie on top and push inside. I'm surprised how wet she is.

She doesn't move so much as an inch, simply lies there, something dead underneath me. I pump away, all the while thinking of Beatrice. Susan's eyes roll back and stare out beyond me into the ceiling. Her mouth hangs half open and she doesn't make a sound, hardly even blinks. After a minute, the blankness only makes me angry. It reflects something inside me, my own blankness after Jaggi's death. I push harder, more violently, and begin to pummel her with my body, my flesh slapping into hers, like in those videos Basam watches. I've not healed yet and my muscles wince from the pain. The small cot shakes and the harsh slaps fill the room, and no doubt the corridor outside. Nothing from Susan. Even when her head strikes the wall she just lets her neck bend while her eyes roll back. All I see is an image of myself, slamming into her, of what I've become. A dead man in a dead world. When I come, I hear a small cry rising from her, which she immediately stifles. I begin to pull out but she grabs me and pushes me back inside. We lie like this for several minutes, not saying a word, staring at each other. It's like looking into a freshly dug grave.

Is that how he does it, I say, not meaning it as a question, when she finally releases me, and she nods, and says yes. We're lying pressed against each other on the cot, my back pushed into the wall and hers into me. Our bodies are coated in each other's sweat and I wrap her in my arms. Her bones press into my flesh and it feels almost as if she's not there, that she's somehow vanished. It's how he likes it, she says, and adds that this time she made a mistake, the sound she made at the end. That would have earned her punishment, a punch or lash. A sudden surge of anger washes through me. I hold it in. It's not some deformed woman I should be killing, I think, but him, her guru. No, all the gurus, every last one of them. What right does he have to do this to people? To destroy them like this? I imagine myself throwing him to the floor and slitting his throat. How easy that would be. I'd do it right now if he was in this room. I press her tightly to me and ask if he always comes inside her and she says yes, always, and after he finishes he lies on top of her, the full weight of him crushing her. Only after that does he punch or lash her if she's deviated from what he expected, which is a corpse, she says.

She reaches down and finds a pack of cigarettes under the bed and we sit up and first she offers me one then takes one for herself. I find the lighter on the windowsill and light them both. There is little here of the Susan that I remember from Paharganj. It's hard even to look at her, to look at what he's done to her. Gone is the ceaseless chatter, the wide-eyed enthusiasms, the madwoman talk of our linked destinies. She's hardly said a word since I entered. I miss the other Susan, the one that still had other paths before her, not just this, this living death. I watch as she smokes the cigarette down to the filter, letting the ash drop to the floor, then crush the butt under a bare foot. I crush mine on the windowsill and carelessly flick it across the room. She smiles when I do that, and traces the lines of my bruises with her finger. She doesn't ask where I got them. Will you punch me, she says, and I'm not sure what she means, so she says it again. She points to a spot under her armpit. Right here is good, he doesn't hit me often here and he'll be able to see the fresh bruise more easily. At the tip of her finger lingers a faint discolouration, perhaps a week or so old, that fades into the pink of her flesh.

Now? I ask, and she nods. I form a fist and prepare to hit, just the way I'd hit Anders. Hard, she says, very hard. I strike as hard as I can and she flies off the bed and onto the floor. Amazingly, she doesn't let out even a hint of a cry. She staggers for a moment but refuses my hand, then stands and finds her seat on the bed again, next to me, and says thanks. If I wait, it'll be much worse, she says, but now I can tell him you hit me properly, the way he would have done it. On the phone? I ask, and she says, Yes, on the phone. They have a call scheduled for an hour from now. She looks at her watch, which is sitting on the windowsill. One hour and eighteen minutes and twenty-eight seconds exactly, she says. It's a smart watch and instead of showing the time, she's set the face to show a stopwatch counting down. It makes sure she won't miss the call. She hates it now if she misses the call time even by a couple of seconds. These god-men, I say, and make a motion to spit. She stops me with a finger. Don't say that, she says, don't say anything against him, I tell him everything, remember, and if I repeat a word against him, it's not you who gets punished.

51

She makes a phone call and orders beer from the invisible restaurant downstairs. I watch as she slips on underwear and a bra, grimacing at times from the pain because of the sex and the punch. When the knock comes, she opens the door casually and pays the boy holding out the beers. Four large bottles, all strong. I'm still naked, sitting on the bed. The boy glances at me as he accepts the money, and without any expression, pulls the door shut and disappears. I pull on my clothes as she searches for a bottle opener and opens two bottles. I'm sorry for the messages, she says, the urgent ones. She's glad I didn't come when she texted me, it would only have made things messy.

We drink from our separate bottles and she says the first time after her guru beat her she freaked out. It was the first time they'd had sex. She didn't know what was going on, she didn't understand the significance, what he was trying to teach her. She looks at me seriously and says, Everything the guru does is a teaching, even his breath is a teaching. She adds, Sometimes I forget that. I want to say, even when he comes inside you, but hold my tongue. When he hit me that first time, she says, and adds that he really beat her, and beat her badly, with a stick and everything, she ran away to a hotel in town and telephoned her parents in Massachusetts. She was in tears and said all these horrible things about the guru, about how it was all a sham, how he was using her and lying and it was all about sex and who knows what else or uglier things. They booked her a ticket home for the next week. They were so happy, they said, they were going to have their baby girl back.

But I forgot, she says, I forgot the first thing the guru taught me, about truth and power and strength. What if it *was* a teaching, what if he was trying to show me something deeply important. She talks on like this, and mostly I don't listen. I know where it's going, and it's going nowhere interesting. She doesn't catch the flight, she goes back to the guru, her scared parents decide to fly to India. The same old and tedious story. She met them in this room, she says, and laughs, laughs in a sort of nasty, childish way I've never heard in her voice before. They're professors, she says, Dad teaches moral philosophy, Mom teaches political economy, both well known, written all these books and shit. She wanted to scare them, make them walk through the real shit of the world just to see her, show them the real India. She's laughing again, but softer now. The real India, she repeats sardonically, then looks at me, almost startled to discover I'm there. There's only one real India, she says, it's the fist, the fist in the face, and either it's your fist, or the fist is in your face, that's what my guru says, that in the end there is nothing but the fist, that is the beginning and the end of his teaching, he once said, the teaching of the fist.

When her parents walked into the room she didn't say a word, not one word the whole time they were here. She sat mute as they talked and pleaded with her and cried. It was what her guru instructed her to do. She simply sat on the bed and stared forward, as if they weren't there. After an hour, she stood up and stripped her clothes off, even took her underwear off, and turned a series of slow circles in the middle of the room. She wanted to show them, she says, the bruises from the beatings and the marks left from cuts from the whip, how proud she was of them. I know they thought I was crazy, she says, I know they didn't understand, maybe couldn't, not ever, but I had to try, try to show them how close I was to breaking free from the cycle of birth and rebirth, of life and death. We're both on our second beers, and I think about her parents, sitting in this rotten room, watching their only daughter turn in slow circles, displaying a naked body in agony, a body they probably hadn't seen since she was a child, ravaged by madness. And the truth about power, she adds, the truth about the fist, the fist that is the human world. Her mom was in tears, her dad didn't say a word. He stared at her, like every angry old white man that had ever lived, she says. Then they left, her dad holding her mom in his arms.

She looks at me, suddenly bright eyed, looking more insane than I've ever seen her. I did the right thing, right, she says, showing them who I am, who I've become, what I'm so close to becoming. She corrects herself, *Not* becoming. I say nothing and she talks on. The anger I felt towards the guru drains away and now it's her I hate. How could she be so stupid? How could she let herself be used like this? White, privileged, rich by any standard I know, far more educated. And she throws it away, spits in the faces of parents who love her. Everything about her revolts me. I want to get out of there, away from her derangement, the mania in her eyes, her need for someone to listen, to believe her when she says she's not lost her mind. She talks more about her guru and power and strength and I stand to go but she takes my hand, preventing me, and keeps holding onto it, gripping it with all her strength. I'm close, she says, this close. She drops her beer and lets it roll, spilling across the floor, and presses her thumb and index finger together to show me how close she is, then grabs me with both hands and digs her nails into my skin. Fuck the gurus, I think as I try to pull free, and fuck their mad followers. I want nothing to do with any of them.

The Corpse Sutra, she cries, her voice become high-pitched and urgent, is the last sutra, the only unwritten one, because it is only action, pure action, the words are written by bodies! Her face is pressed into my chest and her arms wrap my torso. The body is the last sutra, she says, shouting, digging her nails into the flesh of my back, before the end, before you lose the body entirely! He says he's never met a disciple like me, so good at the Corpse Sutra, so close, so much like death itself! I untangle myself from her embrace and punch her hard in the chest, again knocking her to the floor, and in three quick strides reach the door when she calls out to me. She's lying on the ground, strangely still, as if frozen, staring up at me, her eyes shimmering yet blank, two dark holes piercing her face. He says soon, she cries out, soon I will be gone, my body not even ashes and my soul annihilated! I race along the hall and hear her voice crying out behind me, Annihilated, annihilated! The words drift in the air as I hurry down the stairs and back into India, real India or whatever this country is, the fetid air of her guru's fist blasting into my face.

52

An auto blares its horn in the tight alley and I jump out of its way. I check my phone. More messages. From the Big Man, from the Captain, one from Beatrice. I ignore the others and look at Beatrice's message. It reads: Will you still do it? Tomorrow night? I type instantly: Yes. Seconds later she sends me back a pulsing heart emoji. I don't know what changes my mind, what makes me decide to do it after all. I walk quickly, searching for a knife store. I can't stab her in the belly, I think. With all that fat who knows how long it will take for her to bleed out. It will have to be quick, a slash across her neck, just like what those fuckers did to Jaggi. Thinking this pushes

Susan and her talk of power and fists and gurus and real Indias out of my mind. Maybe that's why I said yes. I'm happy to leave Susan behind with her trailing cries of annihilation. The last thing I want to think about is the madness of young women caught in the lies of gurus. Concentrate on the task at hand. Make money, get out of this city. It's what Jaggi would want me to do. As I push through the alleys, night begins to fall. Despite the lights of fish mongers and snack stalls, all I see are the growing shadows in between, the stretches of road and wall and alley where what lingers is an empty chasm, the kind of darkness I might finally call my true and natural home.

53

Anders is where I left him hours ago, face almost pressed into the river of red flowing across the screens. I walk past the open office door towards the bedroom and he doesn't hear me, or if he does, pretends I'm not there. I stash the knife in the underwear drawer. After I bought it, I had it sharpened again, just to make sure. I want the death to be quick. I can already see her lying there, in the dark, blood pooling on the grass from her slit throat. There's another message from Beatrice. Everyone's happy, she writes, meet tomorrow before. I send back an ice-blue heart emoji, and collapse onto the bed. I wake hours later, in the middle of the night, still smelling of sex, of sweat, of Susan. I take a shower and shampoo my hair. The steaming hot water feels like a revelation against my scalp. I let it rain down over me, pouring off my body, splashing at my feet. If I stand here long enough, maybe I'll melt, like a pillar of mud, and drain into the sewers of Delhi and out into the vast oceans of the world.

I dry myself and dress and find Anders still sitting where he was, but now pushed back in his chair, staring clinically at the three screens. He glances at me and tells me to come in and pull up a seat. I've been trying to talk to it, he says, and corrects himself, to him, to her, to you. Trying to find some basic language, some form of communicating. His voice is thin and laboured. He's not even sure if it understands the concept of language, the concept of communication. Maybe it's only a baby, he says, maybe the only way it can communicate is through gesture, through bawling, but how does an AI life-form make a gesture. He wonders what would happen if he releases it, if he introduces it to The Atlas. The exhaustion is obvious on his face. He looks as if he's barely able to keep his eyes open. What would happen? I ask, humoring him more than anything, sensing more and more a frail cry at the edge of his madness. He gestures to the screen. This, he says, and laughs. It's a silly laugh. He adds, You, his laugh now sounding oddly like Susan's. He takes my hand and looks me in the eyes. You, he says, still laughing. You. I pull away, overcome again by exhaustion. I want the night to engulf me, lift me up and carry me away. As I walk towards the bedroom, I can hear him laughing. *You, you, you!*

54

I'm swimming, but the water's not dark, it's blue, clear and bright and blue. It's like I'm flying through the air. Shafts of sunlight slice through it, brightening my body as I move forward, illuminating schools of multicoloured fish. There is no sunken ship, no drowning figures struggling to be rescued, just water and light, blue and clear. I swim and keep swimming. When I wake I'm puzzled by the strangeness of the dream. I've never had one like it. I dress and find Anders still in his office. He's hunched over the desk, asleep. Something bizarre has happened to the screens. Instead of red, they're all blue, bright, glittering blue, like my dream. A river of blue flowing across three screens, from one side to the other. I don't have time to wake Anders and ask him. I'm already late to meet Beatrice.

55

We meet at the pastry shop, the one where we ordered half the menu. This time we order only coffee. The manager looks disappointed. He approaches a couple of times, making one suggestion or another. Finally, I look up at him and say, I hate sweets, I always have. He backs away, hurt blossoming across his face. Beatrice suppresses a smile. She's changed her hair, put gel in it or something, so its spiky. It makes her look more intimidating than usual. A new perfume too. It fills the room. We talk mostly of things that don't matter, or I listen as Beatrice talks. I don't tell her about Jaggi, I don't want to tell anyone. And I don't have anything else to say. She tells me the Big Man is making plans to restart the operation, different name, same deal. He wants me to head it this time, design it from scratch, the training, the methods, all of it. I'll have a bigger stake in the profits, much bigger. He has other plans for her. She doesn't say what those are. She asks if Jaggi's still on board and I say yes, he'll be with me tonight. That's true, I think, except his body won't be there, it'll be wherever it is, rotting into soil or concrete.

What are you going to use? she asks, and I say, Knife, and she nods. I add, It's sharp, made sure, the throat, so it's clean. I've rehearsed this part of the conversation a dozen times in my head, though why I'd need to practice for Beatrice I don't know. Maybe I'm practicing for myself,

trying to prove I am the killer I am about to become. All
cool? she says, and I nod, All cool. She reaches out and
places a hand over mine. The Big Man might be a dick,
she whispers, but that woman, she doesn't deserve to live,
she's a waste of space in a way too crowded city. Sure, I say,
and realise I want to change the topic, if a conversation
is what we're having. She asks if I want to do some lines,
and I shake my head, no, I want a clear head. So what is it
you'll be doing for the Big Man? I say, and she says she's
not supposed to talk about it, but she will, seeing as it's
me and I'll no doubt hear about it soon enough.

She drops her voice to a whisper again and strokes
the back of my wrist. The elections, she says. She says
it like that's all she needs to say, but I give her a dumb
look and she rolls her eyes. The elections, she repeats.
So what about the elections? I say. What do you think?
she says, the Captain and the Big Man, and guess who,
you know. I don't know, I really don't. She calls over to
one of the waiters and asks if they have a copy of today's
newspaper, any newspaper really. He returns a minute
later with one. She flicks quickly through it until she lands
on a photographic spread showing some chief minister or
bigwig type inaugurating a new highway project. What
you did, Special Agent Bob Masters, she says, it got a lot
of attention. This man, she says, pushing a finger into the
bigwig's face, and people close to him. And this is about
the elections? I say, and she says, Yes and no, elections,
politics, the future, a strong India standing proud in the

world. She grins, And of course, money, more money than either of us could ever dream of. I hear Susan in her voice suddenly, just like I'd heard it in Anders. It's so jarring that I don't know what to think.

I tell her I don't care one way or the other, she can have whatever India she wants. Maybe that's why I like you so much, she says, you don't believe in anything. What's there to believe in? I say. She moves her hand and unzips my jeans and slides her hand into my underwear and takes hold my balls and starts to squeeze, harder and harder, all the while looking straight into my eyes. Power, she says, that's all there is. The table is small, in the centre of the room. Everyone can see what she's doing. I watch the staff visibly stiffen, unsure how to respond, along with a handful of customers with a direct view. Beatrice doesn't move her hand for over a minute. Neither of us say another word, not until she releases me and says, I really like you.

We pay the bill and the manager approaches, attempts to say something, blubbers a few incomprehensible sounds, and quickly retreats. The staff follow us silently with their eyes as we walk out and as the guard opens the door he gives us his most stern look, the you're-never-coming-back-in-here look. Once outside, she tells me she has something to give me. She pulls a brown envelope from her purse and slips it into my pocket. Half the money up front. There's one plane ticket inside, flying south, leaving tomorrow morning. She'll meet me at the airport. She's booked a house for a couple of weeks on a beach in Kerala. The sea, the sun, the sand, she says. It's Jaggi's dream, I think, made flesh, but I don't say that. We'll swim every day, she promises, then we'll get ourselves nice and fucked up. What about Jaggi? I say, and there's a moment of hesitation before she says, as bluntly as she can, Forget him, he's going to be a star. She kisses me on the mouth, sliding her tongue between my lips. And you're going to be a hero, she says, my hero. She laughs and walks away. I watch her cross the parking lot and walk into the street. For a couple of seconds the light breaks through and catches her hair and makes every motion of her body lithe, almost joyful, and I think of the sun and the beach and the blue water, the water I'd been swimming through in my dream only hours earlier. Was it this, were my dreams telling me, were they making a promise, would we somehow save each other? I hail an auto-rickshaw and give directions back to Anders' place. Or was it a warning? I climb in and the motor clacks to life and I feel again the choking stranglehold of Delhi's air.

56

In the auto, I play it over in my mind. I walk forward in the dark. I see her. I see the surprise. By then it's too late.

I'm behind her, the knife is out. I grab her head with one hand and with the other slice through her throat. She falls and before the blood can touch the grass I'm running. Running for the gate, for the street, for whatever freedom it is a murderer enjoys. Over and over as the auto races through the darkening day.

57

Anders is awake, smelling like he's showered, and he has shaved, sitting drinking a large mug of coffee at the desk in the office. What time is it? he calls out, when he hears me shut the front door. I tell him and stand leaning against the doorway, staring at him, the screen, his strange world. I can't get the image of him as the headmaster out of my head. Is that who he really is? Just another headmaster exploiting the world to feed his sexual frenzies? The screens are still blue, washing from right to left. We both stare, mesmerised, and I tell him about my dream and waking up and finding everything changed. I told you, he says, it's you. I still don't understand what he means, and I doubt he does either. Is this about the elections? I say. I pull up a chair and sip from his coffee. It's strong. It's about much more than any election, he says, nodding towards the screen. Power, I say, and money? He laughs, Yes. He runs a hand across my thigh and asks how I'm feeling. Better, I tell him, and he says I shouldn't worry, I can stay as long as I like, he's got used to having me around.

I take a shower and find the knife. It's a simple wood-handled kitchen knife, one of the cheap ones available in any general store. When I had it sharpened, I kept asking the man to make it sharper. He laughed when he handed it back. The sharpest blade in Delhi, he declared. I test the edge against my thumb. The slightest touch causes a bead of red to erupt. I wrap it in a cloth rag and slip it into my back pocket. I'll open the door, walk across the grass, find her in the dark, and approach from behind. I study myself in the full length mirror, and tell myself I'm looking at a killer, Jaggi would be proud. I'll slice her neck open and watch her fall, and before the blood hits the grass I'll be running. I do jumping jacks in front of the mirror, the way Jaggi used to do them, then thrust my fist at it, yelling, Ha! Ha! Ha! I'll keep running, past Beatrice, past the Big Man, past all of them, past my whole stinking life. I stretch my hands high over my head, breathe in, breathe out. I hear Anders calling. He must have heard me yelling.

It's red again, he says, when I walk into the office. The change happened minutes ago. A few lines of blue continue to struggle amongst the red, my dream of this morning fighting to stay alive. He tells me in this version, The Atlas, *his* Atlas, is gone, it's been erased, buried, drowned, he doesn't know the word. It's become something new. This red, I think, is no longer Jaggi's red but her red, her blood, the Big Man's sister's blood spilling across the grass and overflowing onto the screen. It will follow me all my life. When the government has The Atlas, I say, when it's finished and you give it to them, what will they do with it? He laughs. Anything they want, everything, it's power, pure power.

Without asking, he unties my belt and drops my pants and underwear and takes me into his mouth. Once again, it feels like a violation. I think of Susan trapped in her shitty hotel room, and her parents, their destroyed hearts, her monster of a guru. I don't know why, but that image of her, trying to grab me, pull me back into her room, it fills my vision. Anders works my cock and the red on the screen pulses, while the few strands of blue grow brigher. I pull his head back and look down at him. What would happpen, I say, if you put *this* into The Atlas—I point to the screen—if you put me into it? Would I take over like I'm taking over here, would it all go red like this, would I become India, would I become India's dreams? He says nothing and returns to his task and I watch as his head moves mechanically like a piston. I don't feel much of anything, certainly not pleasure, just his distant, almost sickening compulsion. Anders' single-minded absorption repels me and I want nothing more than to get out of there, get out now. I pull out of his mouth and he looks up confused. What are you doing? he says, and rubs a hand along my thigh, smiling broadly, weirdly. He kisses the tip of my penis. You know you're already India, he says, my secret India, there's no other India I need. I don't want to be anyone's India, certainly not Anders'. I walk into the bathroom and wash myself for the second time in an hour. When I return he fails to notice I'm there. He stares blankly at the screens, lost again in his dream India, in what he believes is me.

58

I repeat it, a mantra. Open the door. Walk across the grass. Surprise her from behind. Slit her throat. Run. Open the door. Walk across the grass. Surprise her from behind. Slit her throat. Run. Open. Walk. Surprise. Slit. Run. And playing behind the mantra is another voice, Beatrice's, telling me she deserves to die, that if there is one body in this stinking city of Delhi that wastes too much oxygen, it's hers.

59

The auto driver drops me off a quarter mile from the house. The streets are mostly empty, wide blank spaces across which a few speeding SUVs scream their presence. The parked autos are darkened by the shadow of drivers snoozing across back seats. Guards warm themselves over fires in the cool night air. And dogs, awake, asleep, roaming, sniffing. If Delhi in the day belongs to people, it's dogs who own the city at night. I walk quickly, along a wide avenue, in the street to avoid the jagged pavement, then turn and find the wall. For some reason, there are tears in my eyes. Maybe somewhere deep inside I'm thinking of Jaggi. I'm always thinking of Jaggi. It's like he's right here, walking with me, always beside me. The wall is buried under dense layers of foliage. Across the street, at the new mansion, there's a party underway. Someone's getting married. Strings of light stream down along the façade while music blares and a DJ shouts into his mic, his voice distorting. The guests have spilled out into the street and a spotlight fans across them. For a moment it lights me up, then passes on. I think of calling Beatrice, asking her if I should abort. A week from now I doubt I'll have the courage, or the will, to go through with this again. The mantra rings in my head. It's now or never.

I pull the vines free and check the lock. The door swings open when I push it. The metal creaks, but any sound is drowned out by the blare of the music. I unwrap the knife and drop the rag to the ground and press forward, into the garden. The grass is wet, recently watered. I can see the house. It's dark except for a handful of lights on the upper floors. I follow the wall to my right, where most of the trees stand. Their branches catch the glow from the spotlight. I move from tree to tree, keeping low, circling through the garden. It's larger than I remember. Then I spot her. She's not too far away and talking into her phone. The side of her face is lit by the glow from the screen while one hand grips the cross bar of her walker. I move closer, to behind another tree, and soon I can hear her complaints about the wedding, the music, the lights. There's a tree even closer I can easily circle around to, so I can approach hidden with my knife. On the phone she's not only distracted but can't move easily. It's all too simple.

I move from tree to tree until I'm nearly level with her. I see her now more clearly. The bulk of her, her straining to hold herself upright, even with the walker, and in momentary flashes, glimpses of her face when the spotlight passes by. It's whiter than I remember. The creams she uses look like they've turned it to chalk. Ugly, defaced, hideous, the whiteness of her skin worse than a mask, closer to a deformity. I'll be putting her out of her misery. The mantra sings in my head. Walk across the grass. Surprise her from behind. Slit her throat. Run. I grip the knife more tightly. It feels like a destiny. All that's left is to circle behind her and finish the job. I begin to advance in her direction when I see what looks like a shape moving quickly across the grass.

I wait and watch. It's the dog, Maxim. It runs up to her and jumps onto her legs. She ignores it and keeps talking, and soon I can hear it whining for attention. A sharp, thin whine bleating faintly under the sound of the music. This stupid dog, she says into the phone, the bloody thing poops everywhere, there's not a day I don't walk in this stupid dog's shit. She kicks it with her foot, but can't muster any force. The dog thinks she's playing, and gets excited. Get away, she cries, get away! She kicks harder, and this time succeeds. The dog retreats, then notices me, and approaches cautiously at first, then more quickly. Beatrice was right. The dog doesn't bark at strangers.

Maxim jumps onto my leg and whines, wanting my attention now. Why didn't Beatrice warn me the dog might be out? I reach down to pet him, hoping to silence him, but he lets out a single, sharp bark and retreats. Instantly, the sister looks across in my direction. Dog, she says, then seems to see me. Hello, is someone there? Hello? I don't move. I just watch her. She switches on the flashlight on her phone and points it in my direction. The beam is too weak to reach me. Hello, she says, then her tone changes, Oh, come closer, no wait, he pooped way back there. She indicates a spot with a nod of her head. Go on, don't stand around, find it and clean it up, I don't want to be stepping in it tomorrow, use your hands if you have to. I take a step towards her. There's no need to surprise her from behind. She's not going anywhere. She gripes into the phone, These bloody servants, they stand around all bloody day, not one of them does a thing, you'd think they should be paying us. She looks at me again. Well, go on, get it now, don't stand there.

She points the flashlight at me again and I raise the knife and let the blade glint, reflecting it back into her eyes. Now is the time to do it. I am the knife, I tell myself. In that moment, I become it. I walk quickly, Maxim whining louder and louder. A shock of recognition crosses her face and she drops the phone. I can hear a distant voice asking where she is, what's happening. She begins to let out a thin, strange whine, similar to the dog's, and grips hold of the walker with both hands and tries to move. She can't, she's paralyzed. I'm feet from her. The spotlight cuts across the garden and comes to a stop, illuminating both of us. She screws up her eyes, trying to get a clearer look. I know you, she says, the young man, my brother. Her voice trails off. Then she remembers. Prince Valiant, she says, the hero of the day. Her face is lit up and I can see it in all its disfigurement. The creams have given birth to a ruptured landscape of discoloured flesh, a horror with white and grey and endless, sickening tones erupting across it. She looks like a ghost, already dead and gone, her face a bleak, gleaming disk.

I don't say a word, I look at her, and then I see her eyes. Small, terrified, lost. My brother, she says, my brother sent you. The last words of the mantra repeat in my head. Cut her throat, let her drop, run. I smell urine in the air and see her trembling, tears running down her face, her body become jelly. My brother, my brother, she repeats. She drops to her knees and lets out an agonised, guttural howl, but almost silently, as if she's afraid of bringing anyone out, of having servants watch this moment, how her life ends, the humiliation of it. She sounds like a child being crushed under a rock. There's something vile in her debasement, in how misshapen she looks, throwing her arms high, her body twisted into awful shapes. It shifts something inside me. I'm as moved as I am repelled, by her plight, her terror, the fear I've brought into her eyes. I think of Jaggi, of the moment the knife sliced across his throat, and realise I can't, I can't kill this woman, however much she might deserve it, however appalling she is or is not. She's too pathetic, letting out that sickening, low wail. I take the knife and throw it towards her. It bangs against the foot of the walker and lands on the ground, near her knees. She looks down at it in confusion. I don't wait to explain. I turn and walk away. The mantra in my head goes silent and I feel my feet on the earth, walking across soft grass. I'm thinking of Jaggi, I'm always thinking of Jaggi, of his arms, his body, his lips, his sweat, his smell. As I walk away, he walks with me.

Behind me, she's found her voice and starts to scream. Murderer! Murderer! I ignore her and walk towards the door. The music grows louder, and soon I can't hear her anymore. I catch a final glimpse before I push back out into the street. Her hands are flung high, her head thrown back in a wild angle, her mouth wide and tortured, and in the distance the dog, a tiny white blotch, staring in confusion at it all. She looks like one of those drawings of crazed Christian saints I remember from old books, at the moment they're burned on a pyre. When I reach the wall the dull thud of the wedding bhangra buries everything else. I walk through the door and into the street, leaving the door swinging open. The party is wilder than ever, people pouring out in all directions. Someone punches someone. Someone grabs a chair and brings it down on someone's head. It's not a real wedding until there's blood on the ground, or so I remember hearing once. I think it was my father who said that. I move briskly on, sidestepping the commotion, along the wide, unruly street.

60

The phone buzzes in my pocket. I'm sure it's Beatrice, and I wonder what I'll tell her. That I couldn't do it, that I didn't want to, that maybe I don't understand a thing about life but for a moment understood something about pity, about loss, maybe even about love. I can already hear her shouting at me, Go back, go back and kill the bitch! The phone stops and I walk half a block and it buzzes again. More insistently this time, as if it's willing me to dig it out of my pocket. I'm suddenly overcome with exhaustion and want to drop to the ground right there, lie on the pavement and simply stop and wait for whatever happens next. My will's broken, maybe it's always been broken, and seeing her ravaged face, the hunger for money, for status, for poisoning her brother's life written all over it in that tortured white mask, all I saw was myself, Beatrice, the Big Man, our big unhappy future family. I remember the moment I walked out of Susan's squalid room and decided to kill the sister. Susan's madness was painted across every face and street of Delhi, screaming back at me. What if I was wrong, what if all I saw was myself. I don't stop, I keep moving, my body does it against my will. The sound of the party grows faint and police sirens rise in the distance. I don't change my pace and the phone buzzes again. This time I look at the screen. It's not Beatrice, it's Anders. No doubt the colours on the screen have changed again and he wants to know why, what happened. I ignore it and walk on, thinking of Anders and his map. What if he's right, what if he's not a madman? What if he has made me India, the dreams of India? Is the madness I saw in his face my own? I walk forward into the night, into the city, and think of her, the sister, on her knees, beseeching the blind heavens for help when she should be beseeching me. I would save her, I'd hold out a hand that held in it a soul or conscience, whatever it is she's missing, who knows, the tiniest drop of love, and give it to her, press it deep into her chest, until the warmth floods her body. I'd become a djinn and fly across the night and the world carrying Susan home and drop her, just as she is, naked and wretched and drunk, back into her bedroom in whatever cold Northern town she was raised in, and wait long enough to watch the surprise on her parents' faces. I'd transport Beatrice back in time, I'd give her back her name, Kavita, and travel all the way to when she's a baby lying in a crib, her diapers being changed by an ayah, and wait, and watch, year after year, decade after decade, I'd be India, Dream India, standing over her like a guardian, saving her from the day she meets the men in that movie. The phone buzzes again. It could be any of them. Anders. Beatrice. The Big Man. I don't look. I'm not sure I ever want to hear any of their voices again. There are no Dream Indias, there are no Prince Valiants, not me, not anyone. And Jaggi is dead. He is dead now, and he is dead a thousand years into the future. Ten thousand. A million. The fog thickens and far ahead, lit by the fast-moving headlight of an auto, the haze brightens and outlines in silhouette several figures, distant shadows in the mist. I walk towards them, thinking of Jaggi's arms wrapping me. He is always dead and his arms are always wrapping me. The auto bursts out of the fog, its cyclops eye sending shards of light in all directions, a sudden visual cacophony. It shoots past me and disappears and I keep walking, feeling the cold embrace of a Delhi night.

Acknowledgements

The initial draft was started in Athens, Greece, the majority written at the Sangam House Writers Residency in Bangalore, and completed in Fort Kochi. Thank you to Sangam House's organisers and staff: Trupti, Ravi, Veronica, Rohit and Jahid, and to my fellow residents: Abdul Rasheed, Purnima Tammireddy, E. Santhosh Kumar and Amulya B. Special thanks go to Arshia Sattar and D.W. Gibson, the Sangam House directors, and the administrator Dhruvatara, who read an early draft. At Westland, V.K. Karthika read and supported this work from the earliest versions. Thank you to all the folk at Westland, especially Amrita Talwar, Avdyushka Gupta, Shivani Kaul and Saurabh Garge.